My Dog Trainer is a Werewolf, I Swear

Jayna James

Published by Boldmerth Publishing, 2024.

MY DOG TRAINER IS A WEREWOLF, I SWEAR

First edition. January 12, 2024.

Copyright © 2024 Jayna James.

ISBN: 978-0986963247

Written by Jayna James.

Table of Contents

For Robin. You know what's funny.

Prologue

The sudden loud rattling of the front door of the *Friendly Potions Shop* jolted Althea out of her doze behind the ancient cash register. Her heart pounded for a moment before her head cleared. Someone had tried to enter, shaking the door hard enough to cause the inside bells to tinkle. She waited. The ticking of the old clock, with a tiny magpie instead of a cuckoo peeking out, hammered the silence for several seconds. 10:56 - almost an hour past opening.

She didn't care – depression fogged her mind these days. She sighed and thought about making some tea, but couldn't decide which kind: peppermint to soothe her senses or cinnamon to stimulate it?

As she let her thoughts drift, she heard the clamoring of magpies behind the shop. They were loud and relentless, determined, those meddlesome birds.

The old cushion in the chair retained the shape of her bottom after she heaved herself out and waddled through the dim narrow space, past shelves of plain jars, bottles and exotic containers, past the large storeroom, all the way to the back door. The soft click of the deadbolt caught the sharp ears of the magpies. Their answering shrieks grew closer. She knew they flew down from the high electrical pole and alighted on the ground outside the door.

She turned back to the storeroom, where she kept more of her herbs and elixirs – the special, rare ones - as well as a small microwave, bar-sized refrigerator, and her laptop computer. She pulled four cans of soda from the refrigerator and set them down on the round table

---

in the center of the room. At the back of a shelf, she found a green jar filled with the luminescent flakes of her exclusive revitalizing remedy and sniffed it. Even the scent made her feel better.

She had just settled herself into one of the hard chairs when she heard the hinges of the back door creaking open; then the clacking of high heels attacking the old linoleum. The door banged shut. The heavy smell of earth and pine drifted in ahead of the visitors.

"Althea! Why is the front door locked? Are you in a spell?"

Three women, all smartly dressed in creamy white silk blouses, billowy black trousers and shiny black shoes filed into the room. They moved with straight spines and an air of robustness Althea missed.

They were sisters, but aside from their clothes, they did not resemble each other. Cricket was the oldest, the one who had spoken. Square-bodied and square-faced, with short platinum hair gelled out in spikes, she plunked down in a chair and smiled brightly as she flipped open the tab on one of the cans. She took up the jar and shook some of its contents into the soda. The other two did the same.

"Maybe she's hiding because she didn't want us to see her dressed like that," said Marian, five years younger than Cricket. She was shaped like a large-bottomed pear and had rather black hair pulled up into an untidy little ponytail on the top of her head. Her small eyes gave Althea's faded green satin pajamas and pink rabbit slippers the once over.

"Don't be so tactless," Cricket scolded. Marian looked away.

Georgine, the youngest by several years, drained her can of soda and licked her lips before she spoke. "Is it a spell? Tell us." She was skinny and her little eyes glanced hungrily toward the refrigerator.

Althea was the oldest and had the most experience in otherworldly activities, which was why she did not want to tell them her problem, why she needed to avoid them. What was happening to her was too demeaning, not to mention worrisome.

The frown line between her brows deepened and she let out a sad huff of air. "My time is over," she admitted at last. "I'm losing my 7th Sense."

"No..." Georgine said quickly.

"Oh, sweetie, I'm sure you're just tired," Cricket assured her.

Althea gave them a look of anguish and pointed to the floor under the microwave trolley in the corner where many black ants scurried in random patterns. "I've been telling them to leave for days."

The three friends gaped. After a moment Georgine flicked out her hand and snatched one. She held it up to her eye.

"Don't you dare eat it," Cricket warned.

Georgine snorted, her eye still on the ant. "Depart," she said and tossed it back on the floor. With that, all of the ants stopped their frenetic motion and in a single line disappeared under the door.

Althea's lips trembled. Marian patted her arm. "Cricket is right. You could be coming down with something. Or perhaps you need a holiday to recharge?"

Althea wanted to believe her. "I've been invited to cook for Paloma's boys for the summer while she and her husband visit Greece. I can't be like this there. They may require my help."

Cricket shifted her position, her silk blouse rustling like feathers. "You will be fine. The change of air will realign your senses and by the time you get back, you'll be even stronger than before."

"You don't understand. I think Tony will need me for more than just cooking. Or somebody will."

Georgine raised a brow. "Is something wrong there?"

"Well, that's the problem, isn't it? My 6th sense tells me something dark is on its way. I was trying to reach into the 7th realm this morning, and I guess I dozed off."

"Hmm. Perhaps if we helped?" Without waiting for permission, Cricket cocked her head listening into the atmosphere and her eyes became round and huge, as if she peered into a cave. At the same time, Marian's and Georgine's heads moved bird-like from one position to another, testing all directions. Their antics continued for several minutes until a muffled warning growl surrounded them. Althea felt coarse fur brush her face. She jumped and touched her cheek.

Her sisters jerked, concentration broken, and stared at her. "Well, that came through loud and clear, didn't it?" Georgine said. "You have no choice. You must go to Paloma's boy. And no more talk of losing your 7th sense. You have work to do."

Marian reached across the table and took one of Althea's hands in hers while Georgine took the other. A flutter of energy passed from them to her but...was it enough?

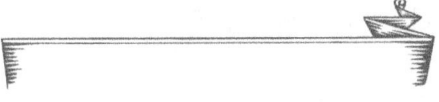

Chapter 1

T he sudden cry on the other side of the door to the Alpha Guy Dog Training Center was neither human nor canine. It started low and rose a scale for several chilling seconds before dropping into a soft tortured moan. Then a thump, like something fell to the floor.

I froze, my heart thudding. Big Jake stiffened, ears forward and hackles up. As the moaning died away no other noises cracked the eerie silence until a car door creaked behind us.

Shannon got out of her white sedan and slammed the door. She was still trying to blot wet spots from her baggy t-shirt and the front of her jeans with a used tissue from her purse. We had driven all the way from our house with the dog's rump in the back seat and his grey head between us, bad breath and drooling tongue close to Shannon's right ear. Her commands to 'sit' did not budge him.

"Don't let my dog slobber problem slow you down," she said, giving me her best stink eye. "Go in."

"Didn't you hear that?"

Big Jake stood nose level to the doorknob, unmoving and intense.

"Hear what?"

"Weird crying."

Shannon tilted her head to listen. Silence.

"Must have been a dog."

"It didn't sound like an animal."

She put her hand on her hip. "Stop stalling. Go!"

"I'm not kidding. And quit giving me orders. I don't think we should go in there."

"Maybe someone needs our help."

"It wasn't an identifiable sound. Too...spooky."

She let out a loud sigh. "Raine, you are so transparent."

"I can't believe you didn't hear that creepy noise," I said.

"Nope." She tried to open the door but it was locked. She pounded on the chipped paint. Nothing stirred.

"Whoever is inside doesn't want any company," I said.

She glanced at her watch. "He's supposed to be here. I called."

"Must have forgotten. He's unreliable already. Let's go."

"I hope you don't give up this easy when training starts." She eyed Big Jake. "You're going to have to work hard with that clumsy dog."

"We're about to pay a stupid amount of money for your sake, not mine. I told you I can train him for nothing. I'd rather buy new clothes for college with that money."

"You don't need more clothes."

I glanced at her mom jeans, her faded brown t-shirt, which was ugly even without the slobber, and her beige hair pulled up in a sloppy bun. My own natural color was the same as hers but my friend Gia had added fine 'sun-kissed' blonde streaks she said brought out the gold flecks in my eyes – also the same color as my sister's only she never did anything to enhance any of her features.

"Your expert opinion?" I said.

"My outfit is more appropriate for dog training than yours. Pale shorts and open sandals? Really? Jake's going to have you dusting the floor with your butt in no time."

I swallowed a retort and rapped on the door again. Something rustled and thumped.

"Sounds like someone fell off a chair. Maybe he drinks. That's what the noise was – he's got a hangover. Let's not bother him." I heard a car start up behind the building and crunch gravel as it drove through the alley.

"I think he just left," I said.

Shannon rolled her eyes and lifted her arm but the door swung open before her knuckles landed. We all jumped, including Big Jake.

A rangy young man with wild thick hair and a day's growth on his pale face pinned us with strange yellow eyes. "Yes?" he said. My 5'3" sister had to tilt her head back to flash her smile and make the introductions.

His eyes flicked from Jake to me to Shannon and back to the dog, then he fingered a two-inch canine tooth hanging from a silver chain around his neck as if it inspired him. He grinned at last, a revelation of largish teeth. "Oh yeah, the girls with the big bad dog." He chuckled and waved us in.

Jake exhibited complete reluctance to move forward, his head down and tail between his legs. I tugged his leash. "Come on, it's okay," I said in my baby doggy voice. "We won't be long."

As Shannon swept in past Yellow Eyes, Jake forced me to drag his 115 pounds past an unblinking judgment. The door banged shut behind us. Jake jumped and flipped around to face him, his hackles up. I'd never seen him so edgy, but then he hadn't been living with us for long.

Only three weeks. I had been walking home from the orchard fruit stand where I worked for the summer when I spotted the huge grey dog in the ditch below the road, a hemp rope tied loosely around his neck and the other end around the waist of an old bearded man. Wearing gumboots and shabby clothes, the man was wading and searching through the cattails, a garbage bag full of empty cans and bottles strapped to his back. The dog had a little grey goatee of his own and was muddy up to his underbelly. When he looked directly at me it was as if he recognized me.

Impulsively I held out my hand to him. He was several feet away, but with enough rope to reach me if he desired. "Hey sir, may I pet your dog?" I called to the old man.

He squinted up at me. "If he wants ya to."

Apparently, he did and climbed the shallow embankment to the blacktop, not fast, testing the air between us with his furry muzzle. I rubbed his neck. He raised his chin and moved his head around, trying to feel the scratch in the largest area possible. We stood like that for several moments.

"I've never seen a dog this big. What breed is he?"

"Wolfhound."

"Is he part wolf?"

The man snorted. "No. He hunts wolves."

"Well, he won't have much to do around here, then," I said.

The man shook his head as if he disagreed. "Don't be too sure about that."

I snickered at the joke. "What's his name?"

Still squinting the man said "Big Jake. Ya like dogs, do ya?"

"I've been wanting a dog since forever but my older sister is scared of them so my parents never got us one."

"Too bad. I'd sell ya this one."

"Are you trying to get rid of him?"

"He's a good dog but he's always hungry."

I moved my hand from the dog's head to feel his torso. No fat.

The dog leaned into me. When I stopped petting him he put his nose to my hand and licked it. I imagined my dog-fearing sister's reaction to this giant.

"How much?"

"$29.95 including five cents return deposit."

I smiled and pulled my wallet from my backpack. It contained exactly one 10-dollar bill and one 20. I held out the money and he hurried up the bank to snatch it from me. He stuffed the bills in a pocket and untied the rope from his waist.

"This dog is meant for you," he said and winked.

"Sure." I smiled and took the rope. "Thanks." With the stately dog at my side, his head up, I walked proudly home. He seemed happy to be with me and didn't look back at the old man once.

Talking to him came as naturally as resting my hand on him. "Shannon is going to have a tantrum when she sees you, Big Jake. But it should blow over after a while if we both ignore her."

Tantrum was an understatement. She shrieked when she saw him, ran to her room, returned and wagged her finger at me from across the kitchen while issuing threats and ultimatums, then stomped out and didn't return for several hours. Then two full weeks of more of the same sputtering and threatening until she started to notice how sweet and kind Big Jake was. She stopped quaking every time he came near but she wouldn't pet him and continued to accuse him of having no manners. Which is why she forced us to the canine training center.

The place smelled of dust and fur and something like rotten eggs which I assumed was the lingering odor of poo. The dim light coming through two small dirty windows gave the room a slightly sinister air. It fell on a few chairs lining one wall and a marked-up old desk near the door. I wondered if the place seem friendlier when it contained noisy dogs and their owners. Now it seemed haunted.

"Are you Alpha Guy?" I knew who he was, but I asked because I wanted him to shut off his weird stare from my dog, and I couldn't think of anything else to say.

He looked exactly like his picture on the big billboard off Highway 97 coming into the city. The ad showed him crouched, going head to head with a Doberman Pinscher, while the text invited humans to learn the language of canines from Alpha Guy, aka Rob Winslow the "dog training wonder boy".

He didn't rush to answer. Instead, he reached for the water bottle on the desk and took a long slow drink. Then he licked his lips, like a dog. "I go by Rob. And you are?"

Shannon took over, like she was afraid I would say something stupid or rude. She explained that I would be the one taking part in the class and how much she'd been looking forward to meeting him given his impressive reputation and she had no doubt that he could help us with our unruly dog. He seemed to like the fawning and a wide grin exposed his longish canine teeth.

He went behind the desk and got a clipboard.

"I heard a sound earlier. Like someone was in trouble," I said to him.

"Yeah?" He didn't look at me.

"What was it?"

"I might have been blowing my nose." He turned away dismissively.

He asked Shannon the dog's name while he checked his list and she smoothed a stray strand of brown hair that had escaped from her tie-back. "Big Jake."

He smiled back. "Descriptive."

"I like Alpha Guy," she said. "The name, I mean." She was so clumsy in her attempt to flirt that I wanted to tell her to stop. But Alpha Weirdo grinned.

"The guys on the police K-9 unit suggested it."

They admired each other for another couple of seconds and then he remembered Jake. Turning his attention to the dog, he made sustained eye contact as Jake growled a low warning. It wasn't the kind of interaction I expected between a dog trainer and a dog.

"He doesn't like you doing that," I said. "He's always friendly with everyone."

"That's because you allow him to be the boss," he said. "Right now he is off balance because has lost his alpha position and he doesn't like it."

Jake's growling increased and Shannon's eyes widened.

"That can't be good," she said in a hushed tone.

"He's not bad," I snapped. "Rob is making him do this."

Rob folded his arms and studied Jake as if he was looking at a bug specimen. "Hmmm. How long have you had him?"

"Three weeks. Raine found him in a ditch and decided to bring him home without checking with me first."

"He's an amazing dog," I was close to shouting.

She rolled her eyes. "She claims we need a big dog to protect us while our parents are away. But as it turns out, we need protection from the dog. He jumps up on our beds while we're sleeping and if we try to crate him, he whines. If we put him in the back yard he sits at the door and howls. He has a bottomless pit for a stomach. I think we've already spent $100 on food for him."

"$50," I interrupted. "My money."

She ignored me. "In the house, he slobbers and doesn't go away when told to do so, he stares, he gets in the way, he chewed up my favorite running shoes..."

Rob interrupted her rant. "I get it. He's never been trained at all because of his size and dominance. He's not neutered."

"I can't afford it yet," I mumbled.

"Okay." He put out his hand to take the leash – a bright red leather beauty I bought for my beautiful dog - and then crowded him toward the door away from me. Jake resisted moving and growled again, but Rob didn't pull back, continuing the Alpha Guy stare.

Jake lunged. The trainer dodged the snapping teeth faster than I had ever seen a person move. With a hard yank on the leash, he shouted, "No! You're being rude!"

I reacted instinctively, springing to move between the two of them and tried to catch hold of the leash but Rob moved away.

"I'm not going to allow you to be mean to my dog. We are leaving," I said, too furious to be afraid. I saw something strange about his face, something hard. Jake barked and growled and twisted in his collar.

At last, Rob gave up the leash. "We've got a lot of work to do. A lot of dog owners get worried during the beginning of dog training. This won't last long – once your dog realizes he doesn't have to be in charge anymore, he will actually be happier."

"I'm glad we brought him here before he hurt someone," Shannon said.

I rolled my eyes. My poor Jake was getting a bad rap because of his size. "I thought the best trainers have a rapport with dogs,"

His eyes narrowed. "I train search and rescue dogs, sniffer dogs, law enforcement K-9s. They want to be partners but they are happiest when they understand the rules."

My instincts didn't believe his method made any animal happier. "There are trainers who use positive reinforcement. I want to try that."

"If you want to go somewhere else, go ahead," Rob said. "But if you want the best trainer ask around. You'll keep hearing my name."

To my disappointment, Shannon rushed to reassure him that she had "complete confidence" in him. "Jake needs someone who knows what he's doing."

I felt betrayed, but her focus was on Rob.

"I hate to waste my time if the owner's not on board," he said.

"We are on board," Shannon insisted. "Raine and I will work this out later."

He made a show of thinking things over.

"To tell you the truth, I think Jake could be an amazing working dog for the same reasons your sister can't handle him. He's brilliant and strong. He needs someone who can gain his respect in order to live up to his potential. I'll tell you what, why don't you leave him with me and I'll commence his training. Only 150 bucks extra. The regular price just for boarding is more than that.

"No way," I said. "He's my dog and I want to learn how to work with him." I turned to Shannon. "No," I repeated.

"Yes, but we made a deal. You promised to get him trained if I agreed to let him stay. Rob, can we wait and see? Raine will work hard with him between classes and if she doesn't make any progress, he'll stay here. The extra money will be worth it, I'm sure."

I couldn't believe what I was hearing. "What?! No! I'm never going to leave him here."

Rob spared me a glance but directed his next question to Shannon. "Can you both commit to working with the dog?"

She explained that she couldn't come to classes because of her job tutoring science and math to gifted students – emphasis on "gifted" - but she would devote herself to Jake's training when she could.

Rob looked skeptical as he regarded Big Jake like a bug in a jar. His hackles were still up and he did not take his eyes off Rob.

I couldn't stand the thought of putting him through even more stress. "You're not connecting with my dog."

"It's a war of wills which I will win," Rob said.

"Raine," Shannon said, "I think you owe it to me to try at least one lesson. After all, I've been a pretty good sport about keeping him."

No she hadn't. She'd done nothing but whine and complain.

Rob looked from me to her then turned to the desk and pushed a form toward her. "Okay, let's get you registered. I'll take an etransfer."

Shannon did as instructed while I stroked my dog and made a point of not looking at Rob.

As we were about to leave he warned us, "You've got a lot of work ahead of you to prove to me that you can control this big dog." He leaned toward Shannon, and I swear he quirked his bushy eyebrows. "I'm placing my trust in you. Don't let me and him - " he gestured to Jake - "- down."

"I really really appreciate this, Rob," she said. She fluttered her eyelashes, something I had never seen her do before.

I couldn't stand the gushing and led Jake outside. After a minute she emerged, a pleased little smile playing on her lips, and we all settled in the car. She ordered Jake "Down!" with more force than usual, and he surprised us both by lying down – so happy to be going, I figured.

"You know what worries me most, Shannon?" I said as the car pulled away from the curb.

She sighed. "What?"

"Your new favorite person just played us."

Chapter 2

Neither one of us spoke for the next couple of miles. I hoped Shannon was thinking about what I'd said. She had always considered herself the smart one so how could Rob have played *her*?

"You're not making sense."

"He used his knowledge of dogs to antagonize Jake, and THEN he made us beg to take us on as clients."

"He thought Jake was going to be a lot of work and he wanted more money for the extra time. That is good business."

I folded my arms. "Some ways are honest and some are shifty."

She smirked. "I think you're jealous because for once an interesting male paid more attention to me than he did to you."

I couldn't let that pass. "Ordinarily I would say he's all yours, but he's too weird, even for you."

"What a rude thing to say."

"Sorry."

Her sideways glance told me she detected the insincerity.

"Why are you so desperate for Jake and me to stay in Rob's training class?" I asked.

"His reputation for results is the best and your dog is the worst. Figure it out."

"The evidence of his skill or lack thereof was right in front of us," I pointed out. Then I tried another angle.

"He stares in a creepy way."

"His eyes are stunning."

"Stunning?"

"Shut up."

I couldn't let it go. "And what about that weird crying sound Jake and I heard? And the thump? I'm sure something was going on before he opened the door. Maybe he was torturing a dog! You could be forcing me to deal with someone who tortures dogs. Don't you have a conscience?"

"Your imagination is out of control."

"You think he's hot, don't you?"

"I'm not interested in him only because he is a good trainer."

"I didn't ask if you were interested in him. Except now I KNOW you're interested in him because you said you're NOT interested in him." I turned back to the window and mused, "Your first love is a dog man."

"A person about to start senior year needs to grow up. Maybe channel all that mental energy into figuring out what you want to be when you GROW UP."

"You're not my mother. You need to grow down."

She rolled her eyes and after that refused to talk for the rest of the drive home.

Our house and apple orchard are nestled in low-lying hills on the north rim of the sprawling city. From the highway at the bottom of our property someone once took a photograph of our orchards sweeping up a gentle slope, all the apple trees in blossom, and digitally added a rainbow arched above the hill to make a postcard. The fruit stand down the road where I worked sold a lot of them to tourists in the summer.

Shannon turned into the drive and the car rolled to a stop in front of our house, a two-story brick with a colorful wave of flowers in window boxes. Her cell phone rang and she hurried into the house.

Jake had been quiet in the back seat of the car but once I opened the door he jumped out and bounced around me, eager for a walk.

It was just after 4 pm. Clouds were rolling in and the temperature had dropped a bit so I decided to take him for a stroll into the orchard before the rain hit. A grass trimmer buzzed not too far away, and I felt a little thrill of anticipation knowing that it must be Tony Callus, the youngest son of our closest neighbors. Dad had hired him to look after the orchard while my parents spent the summer in Greece with his parents.

Jake led the way between two rows of the dwarf trees, their apple-laden limbs straining against the lines Tony had helped Dad tie to hold their weight.

We soon found him. He wore protective eye and ear coverings, and wasn't aware of us until Jake ran in front of him. He turned off the trimmer and removed his headgear. "Hey, Jake." He patted Jakes as guys do to big dogs. Jake wriggled like a puppy until a rabbit took off from a tree near us and he bounded off after it.

Tony smiled, his teeth so white against his dust-covered tan. His shirtless chest gleamed with perspiration.

"Rainie. What's up?"

He was halfway between Shannon and me in age. He had tolerated my presence when we were kids, and later we sometimes hung out with the same crowd in high school but once he went away to college we did not keep in touch.

When he returned for the summer he seemed different. The smile in his dark eyes had changed into something deeper, something that I couldn't put my finger on. And whatever it was, changed things for us. I felt shy around him, like growing up with him had never happened. When Dad announced Tony was going to be taking care of our orchard while he and Mom were away, I was happy. Maybe if we saw more of each other my shyness would go away and we could be buddies again.

"Got a favor to ask," I said.

He wiped his brow with his forearm, "Yeah?"

For a moment I forgot what I intended to say. What was it about sweaty bare-chested guys?

"I need you to show me how to train Jake."

"So you decided against learning from our local celebrity trainer?"

"I'm hoping with your help I can Jake and I can ditch the classes."

He raised a brow.

I kicked at a clump of dirt. "Neither Jake nor I like Rob Winslow."

The sound of a car turning off the road and onto the trail through the orchard distracted us both. A police cruiser appeared from the other side of the trees and bucked slowly along the ruts. When the vehicle came to a stop Tony's brother Nick got out.

I hadn't seen Nick for a year or so since he now had an apartment in the city but he hadn't changed much. Almost three years on the city police force had given him a straighter bearing and shorter hair cut but it was the same old Nick who greeted me like a long-lost family member, wrapping me in a big hug. He was tall and athletically built, a few years older than Tony with the confidence and charm of a guy who knows women like him.

"Raine, look at you. You're a beautiful woman now."

My cheeks warmed. I had known Nick all my life too, but I still didn't know how to respond.

Tony came to my rescue. "What are you doing here, anyway? Shouldn't you be handing out speeding tickets or something?"

"I need you to help tonight at baseball practice. My assistant is sick."

Tony made the hand sign for phoning.

"Mom asked me to look in on Aunt Althea since I'm her favorite." Nick grinned.

Tony snorted. "She may not even like you at all,"

"I'm trying to win her over so she'll give me some of her famous Greek pastry."

"Sure. Well you know I'm always up for coaching your women's baseball team."

"Did I say coach? More like water boy."

Tony laughed.

"Hey, you gotta meet my dog," I said. I called Jake and he made me proud by coming right away. Nick crouched down and held out his hand. "Hello, big guy."

Jake looked up at me.

"Go ahead, he's one of the good guys," I assured him. Immediately Jake jumped on the crouching Nick knocking him over and licking his face.

Tony and I laughed while Nick wrestled the happy dog off and stood up. I grabbed Jake and mildly scolded him, ending with an affectionate kiss on the top of his head. Nick didn't seem upset as he brushed the dirt and grass from his uniform.

"He must be one of those dogs that take a while to warm up to strangers," Tony joked.

As I attempted to apologize Nick stopped me. "He's a good dog. He waited for you to give him permission. That kind of bond is what K-9 officers aspire to with their dogs."

"Well, I think he is pretty great," I admitted. "Wish I could convince Shannon."

He chuckled. "He is a big dog for a little girl like that to handle. By the way, how is Shannon? I haven't seen her for a while."

I heard the warmth in his voice when he referred to her as "a little girl". I was a couple of inches taller than her but she was still my big sister. But he saw her differently, and with fondness. I told him about her science camp for gifted high school students.

"She was always good with kids," he said. "Well, I'd better see Althea now. Tell Shannon I said 'hi.'"

The distant rumble of thunder alerted Tony and me to an imminent downpour. "You'd better get back to your house," he warned.

I said 'bye' and took off at a jog. Jake loped after me and we got home as the first drops hit the ground.

Shannon was in the kitchen making coffee. She turned away from me when I entered. I sat down at the island and Jake found his water bowl. He slurped up a big drink before squeezing into the narrow space between the counter and the island to greet her.

"Get that wet dog away from me!" she yelled, startling both Jake and me. Even she seemed surprised by her outburst.

"What's wrong?"

"Your dog stinks, that's what's wrong."

She turned to look at me and I could see her eyes were red and watery.

"Are you crying?"

"No."

She poured a cup of coffee and avoided looking directly at me again.

I thought about what could have happened since we left the car and remembered her phone had been ringing.

"Did something happen with your job?"

"Get serious." She stirred sugar into her cup.

"So who called you?"

"If you must know, I was supposed to go on a double date with my friend Cassie from work, but the guy she had arranged for me canceled. Therefore, I will be spending my Friday night at home, working on stupid science experiments for the kids, as usual. Happy?"

Not happy, but curious - first flirting with Rob and now a blind date? What was going on with her?

"Dates are canceled all the time. What's the big deal?" I asked, feigning slight disinterest. Always the best way to draw her out.

"He said he had to visit his sick grandmother."

"Maybe he did."

"I overheard a guy in the background yell 'Have you ditched her yet?'"

"Oh." I thought a moment. "Not nice people, sis."

A tear slid down her cheek.

I tried to think of something comforting to say. "Nick Callus was in the orchard just now. He said to say 'hi'."

She ignored the information and started searching the kitchen for a tissue. She found a box in the cupboard and blew her nose.

"Let me introduce you to someone," I said. "In fact, why don't you come out with me and my friends tonight? We can go to that jazz cafe you like." I do not like jazz but I wanted to cheer her up.

Her face turned red. "I am not so hard up that I have to tag along with my little sister."

She didn't need to be so rude, I thought. "But it seems you are."

Angry silence stretched out for several minutes until she finally left the kitchen and hurried upstairs to her room, slamming the door behind her.

Jake came to me and licked my hand, his tail wagging hesitantly.

I patted him. "Is it a full moon tonight or something?"

His brown eyes gazed lovingly into mine.

Chapter 3

That night I had a strange dream which merged into reality in a way that had never happened to me before.

The moon illuminated a faint path between two rows of apple trees as Shannon and I tramped along the grass-scented earth, our bare feet leaving no prints. The porch light on our house twinkled ahead through the branches.

"Faster," she ordered, her voice too loud in the quiet of the evening.

"Who put you in charge?" I said without changing my pace.

She glanced over her shoulder. "I swear the shadows are moving. Why are you so slow?"

"I don't know." I'd observed the shifting shadows as well and I wanted to be home, yet I couldn't make my legs speed up.

The faint howling of a dog in the distance disturbed the silence. Shannon jumped and grabbed my hand.

"That thing sounds hungry," she said. "There's hardly any meat on your bones so he'll come for me."

I shook her off. "Don't talk crazy."

"I'm not..."

All at once a long low wail interrupted us. At first hollow and quiet, the sound gained momentum as more voices joined together in a clamor of keening, moaning and crying.

As it faded away, many paws pounded the ground from all sides. In front of us, at least 10 creatures materialized from behind the trees, giant wolves running toward us with long gleaming teeth dripping saliva. One of them took Shannon in his huge jaws and she screamed. Foul breath blew down my neck and paralyzed me. I opened my mouth to scream.

Nothing came out except a croak, and panic jarred me awake. After a moment my mind cleared and my legs moved at last, kicking the covers off my bed.

Something howled still.

With the pounding in my chest so strong I feared it would explode, I took slow breaths and tried to think rationally. The loudest howling came from the deck off my parents' bedroom. Calm, calm, I breathed. *Jake must be out there.*

A deeper howl rolled across the orchard and Jake answered.

As the beating of my heart slowed to normal, I padded down the hall into the master bedroom. A wall of the heavy valley heat and the smell of fresh-cut hay enveloped me when I stepped out of the cool room and onto the balcony. Jake stood motionless on his hind legs with paws on the top of the railing. With hackles up and ears pricked forward he watched something out where our land butted up to the Callas' farm, even as the distant howling faded. My eyes adjusted to the light of a star-filled sky and half moon, but I could not make out anything in either our property or the pasture beyond. I put a hand on his neck and buried my fingers in his rough fur.

"What's going on, bud?"

He let out a sharp 'woof'. I looked harder, wondering if one of the neighbors' dogs prowled amongst the trees. Instead, a human figure detached itself from the shadows at the edge of the orchard.

My heart resumed its racing. The person faced our house.

I backed into the bedroom and reached for my dad's binoculars from the top of his dresser. On the balcony I trained them on the figure, still motionless, while I felt for the switch beside the door and flipped it. Two high pole lights, one at each side of the orchard, flooded the area and illuminated the features of a lean man in jeans and a tight white t-shirt staring toward the house, his eyes taking on a hollow ghoulish reflection. For a moment surprise rooted him to the spot, then he crouched down and scuttled like a crab behind a thicket of scrub pines.

I gasped, I had seen his face clearly. Rob Winslow. My dog trainer had been casing our property.

I swept the binoculars over the area. A dark four-legged creature flashed between trees in the direction of the trail from the main road and was gone. Jake offered up another deep "woof".

I strained for several minutes to detect where Rob had gone but saw nothing more.

At last, the sound of an engine starting up in the distance prodded me to action and I ran back through the house to Shannon's room, flipped on the light, and pounced onto the bed. She slept deeply, curled up like a baby.

"Shannon, Shannon. Get up. We have to call the cops. Nick. We should call Nick."

A drowsy sigh escaped her lips. "What?"

"Come on. It's an emergency."

She opened her eyes and squinted at me while she processed the information.

"Shannon! Danger outside."

She blinked a few times. Her eyes widened with comprehension and she threw off the blanket. "Is there a fire? Why isn't the alarm on?"

"Rob is sneaking around in the orchard."

She stared at me.

"You know, Alpha Guy."

She continued to stare at me and the binoculars in my hand.

"I'm serious," I said. "We have to call the cops. He could be trying to steal something or...or...do something to us."

"Who again?"

I gave an exasperated sigh. "Rob Winslow. The dog trainer."

"Raine," she whined and got back into her bed. "This isn't funny. Go away."

"Come on! You have to call the cops."

She yelled a few words she doesn't usually say, but basically, she wanted me to remove myself from her room.

"I'm not making this up. Jake was howling so I went outside with binoculars. I saw him, I swear. Rob is out there. We should call for backup."

She pulled away from me and sat up. "Aww...Raine..."

Completely disheveled and angry, she grabbed her glasses from her night table and followed me outside to the balcony. Jake greeted us enthusiastically.

Shannon held the binoculars to her eyes for a couple of minutes before handing them back to me.

"Nope. Nothing."

I pointed out where I'd sighted Rob. "Look harder."

She sighed and tried again. "Oh wait. Yes. The Bogeyman!"

I snatched them and peered out. Nothing, not even a stray cat or porcupine.

"I swear someone was moving around in the trees – someone who resembled Rob. A lot." I was desperate for her to believe me and a whine edged my voice.

"Why would Rob be in our orchard at 2:30 am?"

"Don't know. We'll have to ask him when the police catch him."

Shannon frowned at Jake who gave her a doggy grin and wagged his tail. "Are you sure it wasn't a stray dog? Maybe Jake's kin looking for him? Go back to bed and don't wake me up again unless someone breaks into the house."

She flipped off the switch to the floodlights. "I sure hope the neighbors don't complain about those lights being on in the middle of the night." She glared at me and then strode back inside the house.

I followed her back to her bedroom. "Okay, forget cops we don't know. How about Nick? He'll come."

She turned off her light and slid into bed. "What's he going to do?" She closed her eyes. "You are letting your over-active imagination run away with your brain. Again."

"Aren't you worried even a little bit that someone is casing our property?"

She turned onto her stomach and pulled the pillow over her head. "Stop being a drama queen. If you're that worried about it, let Jake out."

I considered going outside with Jake but also kept thinking about the howling wolf - wolves. Maybe there was a whole pack like in my dream. I kept Jake in my bedroom for the rest of that night – despite the poop risk – but we were both restless after that so I didn't get much sleep.

Chapter 4

My shift at the fruit stand the next day started at 8 am. For a week Jake had been walking me to work and waiting for me in the shade of the awning where I put a pan of water for him. He was so friendly looking with his scruffiness and lolling tongue smile, many tourists stopped to pat his head and one or two even had treats. His tail thumped every time that happened.

Today when I finished at noon we took our usual route home along the road. Just as we turned into the driveway Shannon's car came speeding away from the house and she stopped long enough to roll down her window and yell out, "Going shopping. See you later."

After feeding Jake and stuffing down a quick ham sandwich, I headed out to the area where the intruder had been. Jake galloped ahead of me to a copse of old Macintosh apple trees at the edge of the dwarf trees. He then stopped to sniff around with more intensity than usual.

I spotted some indentations in the grass that could have been footprints and knelt to examine them thoroughly without any idea of what to do next.

A shout from the trail to the Callus farm interrupted my concentration. Tony waved and sprinted toward me. "Hey. I thought we had a dog date."

I told him about our night visitor and the howling.

"No kidding?" He studied the prints. "I know they're not mine." Circling in an ever-widening berth, he soon found more in the thinner grass leading toward the road.

"The soles are patterned – that's a pretty good clue, isn't it?" I asked, thinking about the expensive tennis shoes Rob wore.

"Not enough," he said. "Lots of people wear those. I'll ask Nick to come up here."

A magpie hopped from tree to tree scolding us as we followed the tracks several yards past the sighting area. They disappeared into some high weeds in the ditch and animal tracks appeared on the other side before disappearing at the pavement.

I held my hand flat out over a print bigger than my palm. "Wow," I said. "It must be the howler from last night."

"No wonder Sassy was agitated. These are big enough for a wolf. Can you describe the person? Man or woman?"

I hesitated. "Well...he looked like Rob Winslow."

"The dog trainer? What reason would he have to be out there?"

"Shannon's opinion too. He must have a twin."

He moved purposefully around the prints. "It doesn't make any sense."

He glanced toward his family's property where a large flock of sheep dotted a sloping meadow. "Aunt Althea heard howling last night and launched into her bad omen talk."

His father's eccentric Aunt Althea owned an herbal shop in Vancouver and liked to get away from the city often. My mother once mentioned that for some ailments Althea's cures worked better than modern medicine even though they bordered on hocus pocus. She had consulted the herbalist on a few occasions and insisted Althea's special tea had protected our whole family from colds and flu for many years. I had never met her.

I knew Tony and Nick considered her apparent belief in omens and strange remedies mostly funny but sometimes annoying.

"She makes all misfortunes, big or small, into curses requiring her intervention," he said. "When I was a little kid, she rubbed a dime on a wart I had on my finger, wrapped the dime in a dirty sock and buried it under a full moon in the garden. Since then I never talk about problems around her."

I couldn't help but smile. "Did the dirty socks work?"

"Coincidence."

"I wonder if she's got something for someone who needs a better social life?"

"I'm sure she's got a potion for whatever you want. But I'm surprised you think you need a better social life. Seems to me you have lots of friends. Female and male."

He cast me a sly smile and my cheeks warmed. "Not for me! Shannon."

"Oh. Why are you worried about her?"

"I'm not. Just a joke." His closeness flustered me and I said the first thing that came to mind. "I've never met your aunt but she sounds wonderful."

"She's baking today. Come on up to the house." He grinned, and his eyes promised an adventure like they did when we were kids.

Chapter 5

Jake ran ahead of us in the summer heat, along the crude road through the orchard, effortlessly clearing the wooden fence and off at a lope toward the grey brick house with red roof. Tony surprised me by opening the gate for me but I made no comment. A few years ago he would have let me climb over.

A high cedar fence encircled the back of the house and a dog barked from within. As soon as we entered Jake bounded up to Sassy, a blue merle border collie with blue eyes. They were best friends already although had only met once, and they started to play while Tony and I beamed like proud parents.

I inhaled the cool scent of the Callas's serene turquoise pool. A large umbrella table and chairs beckoned visitors to the shaded side of the cement rim. Jake stopped playing long enough to lap the fresh water dribbling from a statue of a little naked boy.

"Whew, it is a hot day," Tony said, wiping his forehead with his forearm. "I'm going to have a swim. How about you?"

I had no change of clothes so I declined. Instead I sat down at the edge and dangled my legs in the water.

"Come on, you used to jump in with your clothes when we were kids, remember?"

I considered it for a moment but then, "Not in the mood today, I guess." But I wished I could be eight again and feel normal around Tony.

He shrugged and went into the house.

In the meantime Jake and Sassy flopped down beside me in the shade, panting. Jake was so different now than the stressed animal he had been with Rob that I anticipated a productive training session.

"You're a good boy, aren't you?" I said in my mommy doggy voice.

He tilted his head at me with his wolfhound smile while Sassy thumped her tail on the cement. "And you're the best too," I cooed at her.

Moments later Tony returned dressed in baggy orange swimming trunks.

"Auntie is fussing over her pastries, likely planning to eat about five before she brings them out."

I leaned back on my hands and raised my face to the sun. "It is hot."

"Time to cool off!" he shouted without warning and did a water bomb as close to me as possible, drenching me and the dogs. I jumped up and gave in to my inner eight-year-old with a running leap into the water. The dogs stayed back and barked.

Tony dived for me. I tried to escape but he seized my waist and held me with one arm while splashing me with the other. At first I was absorbed in the fun, until I became mindful of the closeness of our bodies, and with burning cheeks I stopped struggling. Aware of my change of mood, Tony let go and I swam back to the submerged steps. He climbed out and went into the house, returning a moment later with towels and a tray of iced tea.

I sat in one of the chairs and tried to dry myself as best I could while Tony took a seat beside me. After a few seconds he whispered, "And here she is." An old round woman dressed in a shapeless black tank top and wide black shorts came through the patio doors carrying a tray of pastries.

She set the tray down on the table and then hoisted her square frame onto the chair closest to me. Tony introduced us and she nodded her head with the barest whisper of a smile. I noticed she kept glancing over at Jake.

"Big dog. Where did you get him?"

"An old bottle picker sold him to me. He said Jake was supposed to be mine."

She studied him like she was trying to recognize him. "Maybe so," she murmured.

Tony handed me a glass of tea and I drank half down in three gulps. Then he offered the tray of pastries. "Have some baklava. Auntie makes the best in the world."

Althea nodded and said something in Greek. Tony was not shy about helping himself to four of them, earning a scowl from her. She chose one and nibbled on it, her expression unreadable.

An awkward silence stretched out between us and I contemplated ways to ease into a conversation about recognizing wolf omens.

Althea seemed to read my mind. "The wolf called last night."

I perked up. "I heard it. And you too?"

"Why do you think it was a wolf?" Tony asked.

"Have you ever heard dogs howl like that?" she said.

I told her about the man in the orchard and the large animal prints we found.

She stared at the hills surrounding our farms. "Not good."

"What do you mean?"

"Wolfen." Her voice was low and dramatic.

"Aunt!" Tony protested. "We're not little kids."

"What's a wolfen?" I asked. A small cool breeze came out of nowhere and lifted the hairs on my arms.

"Werewolf," he said, his face expressionless. He reached for a sixth pastry.

I thought of my mother's respect for Althea's expertise in the use of herbs despite the old woman's odd ways. Althea's belief in the supernatural must have come through experience as well. I couldn't help but give what she said some consideration.

"Is the wolfen dangerous?" I asked.

Tony leaned closer to my ear and whispered, "Don't you..."

Althea ignored him. "He is not a funny movie creature. You should learn about him."

"Auntie, you can't just talk as if your werewolf is real," he said.

She jabbed her finger toward him. "You saw the prints in the dirt, didn't you? Your girlfriend and I heard the howling."

We both blushed at her calling me his girlfriend but Tony did not correct her. I cleared my throat. "What about the man outside our house?"

"There is a logical explanation for everything," he said. "And when I talk to Nick I'm sure he will have a SANE perspective on this."

"Bah! Cops don't have any power in the world of the werewolf." She waved her hand as if trying to make him disappear and heaved herself out of her chair to waddle back into the house.

"You were kinda rude."

He chewed on his pastry as if savoring every bite, then swallowed. "Maybe. But she can be so...what's the word Dad uses? Eccentric. Yeah, eccentric. It's a little embarrassing."

"Maybe ancient stories are about scientific or medical conditions. They couldn't know about things like DNA and genes," I suggested. "Back in ancient times."

"Are you serious? A man who changes into a wolf? Do you think Santa Claus has a medical condition?"

I ignored the jab. "Your aunt's potions do cure things. You don't have anymore warts, do you?"

"Like I said, coincidence."

I said no more as Aunt Althea returned with a plastic container. She opened it under my nose to reveal two little cloth objects the size of tea bags.

"For you and your sister to put under your pillows. They will keep the wolfen from crossing the threshold to your bedrooms. You need not worry."

I was tongue-tied - until a revolting odor wafted up from her gift and I leaned away. "Eew."

The odour reached Tony as well and he erupted into a coughing fit. "What is that?"

Satisfaction settled over her face. She closed the container and set it in front of me.

"Powerful recipe handed down from ancient werewolf hunters, known only to a few," Althea explained.

"Werewolf hunters? Don't you think this is kinda over the top?" Tony said. "Why do you think Raine and Shannon are in danger?"

"The wolf came to them in the night, didn't it? It didn't come to you," she answered. "Raine, do as I say and you will be safe."

"Shannon and I are safe. We have Jake." His ears pricked up at his name and he looked at me "See? He answered that wolf last night. It won't be coming back I'm sure. Besides, I won't be able to sleep with this odor."

"Keep them in sealed containers. The wolfen will still be able to smell." She stared at me. "The wolfen is looking for a mate."

Her matter of fact delivery of such a outrageous claim shocked me. "A human mate?" I asked.

Her voiced dropped. "The wolfen is human too."

"Auntie...you've jumped to this conclusion rather quickly," Tony said.

She pointed a finger toward him. "Video games and artificial intelligence destroys the inner sight. There are other worlds that you suspect are there but instead of exploring them, you immerse yourself in noise."

I was intrigued. "Where are these other worlds?"

She waved her hand. "All around us." She glowered at him, daring him to contradict her.

He put his hands up. "All right, all right. But let's exhaust all natural possibilities before we move into another dimension."

"After all," he continued. "Of all the girls in this part of the world why would a wolfen pick Raine?"

"Or Shannon," I said.

"The wolfen are from another world and we don't know their ways. But I am interested in other explanations for your dog trainer and a large canine their orchard in the middle of the night."

She rose from her chair and addressed me. "Just in case Mr Tony doesn't come up with another reason, keep the wolfen repellent under your pillow. And your sister's."

Awkward. As Tony frowned I had no choice but to agree. Satisfied, she returned to the house.

He watched her go but said nothing more. Instead, he brightened and nodded toward the dogs play-fighting on the grass and smiled. "Okay, break over, time to get serious about training Jake."

Forcing my mind away from Aunt Althea's unsettling words, I turned my attention to Jake. His recall was nearly perfect, and I told him so like a proud mother.

Tony got a bowl of tiny morsels of dried chicken out of the house. He used Sassy to demonstrate basic commands, "sit", "stay" and "up" using positive reinforcement with the treats.

Eager to play the game too, it didn't take long for Jake to learn the basics either.

Tony was pleased. "He's smart and always hungry. You should have no trouble training him to do almost anything."

Both Jake and I enjoyed his approval. And for a while, I put Althea's wolfen talk out of my mind.

I COULDN'T WAIT TO show Shannon the commands Jake had learned, but when I got home, I heard the treadmill humming in the basement and the thud of steps faster than Mom ever ran. Since

Shannon considered a long walk between campus buildings too much exercise, I was surprised she even knew we had a treadmill.

At least her activity gave me time to do what needed to be done with those foul werewolf-repellant packets. I sealed both in air-tight plastic bags and put one under my pillow. To make sure Shannon didn't find hers, I ripped open the seam on one of her pillows, nestled the bag in the middle of the filling, and then hand-sewed the seam back up.

I understood that the likelihood of the existence of a shape shifting wolf man was small, but Aunt Althea was so intense and so sure when she bored her small bird-like eyes into mine. How could she be wrong unless she was crazy and my mother never said she was that. Besides, what could the smelly little things really hurt?

Of course, I did not believe in werewolves as portrayed in books and movies -either marauding biters or as sexy mates. But what had originated the legends? A grain of truth joined conjecture and fueled the stories.

I sighed. Shannon would never appreciate how I agonized over my decision to protect her from an unproven myth, with an unproven pouch of stink that, if discovered, would not go well for me.

Later that evening she went out with some of her science camp students to attend a documentary on "Insect Chemists" so I didn't get a chance to demonstrate Jake's new abilities. I spent the evening researching werewolves on the Internet.

Chapter 6

I arrived early at the Alpha Guy Training Center and only two other dog/human pairs were already there. My resentment at having to be there at all emboldened me to ask Rob if he had been out walking a big dog near our place the night before. He studied me without expression for a moment before his gaze flicked away, dismissing me like a bug.

"Well?" I persisted.

"Hmm? You're a strange girl," he said.

"I saw you," I was shocked at my own recklessness but not enough to back off.

I still believed he had been in our orchard two nights before. Unfortunately, Jake was my only witness and, unable to verbalize his agreement, even though his slinky posture and dropped head whenever Rob approached didn't need an interpreter.

"Be careful about hurling wacko accusations," Rob said in a low warning tone. "You're here to train your dog, right? Let's concentrate on that."

The others were starting to arrive and soon Rob had us paired two by two for a rigorous hike in a local hilly park and back, with hardly any time to enjoy the view of the Okanagan Lake from the top.

"Come on people!" he yelled from the front of the line and smacked his fist into his palm. "The dogs need exercise. If you can't provide it you shouldn't have a dog." He ran without effort, frequently slowing down so the rest of us could catch up, his yellow eyes missing no stumble or lag, at which he would shout out like a drill sargeant.

"Too many carbs first thing in the morning! Eat more like a wolf and you can run like a wolf!"

Everyone was drooping as we made our way back to the cente. The dogs slurped from the fresh water trough outside while us humans drained our bottles. I was panting and sweaty - not my favorite look but I wasn't the only one. Everyone slumped in the chairs, with our canine partners panting at our feet.

But Rob appeared as though he had picked up enough energy for another hike up a hill. He paced in the long floor, his body alpha-straight, eyes darting from one to another. They lingered on me for a moment then flicked away, his expression inscrutible. I wanted to say, "Yeah, I may be the weakest member but I have the best dog!"

Somebody had a farty dog which delivered an odor like a thousand rotten eggs. I detected a few puckered faces trying to pretend the place didn't reek, but Jake's face was impassive. "Probably you," I thought.

Beside me an enthusiastic girl of about 13 stroked her Brittany spaniel, and a tall red-headed boy ordered his hyper hound to sit, without success. I thought that most of the dogs seemed wary - with half-hearted tail wags and watchful eyes.

"I think some of you should sign up for exercise class after this." He smirked. Then he launched into an explanation of how he came to be an expert dog trainer. He had been observing them as well as studying wolves in the wild all his life and learned to think like them and respect their raw beauty and nobility and realized that they understood far more than we give them credit for...blah, blah...People began noticing his way with dogs when he was a teenager and begged him for his secrets...blah, blah...

All the time he talked Jake didn't look at him, instead he stared at the corner of the room behind and to the left of Jake, maybe thinking if he didn't look at the enemy, the enemy would not look at him.

Alpha Guy wagged a long finger at his students. "The number one thing to remember throughout these coming weeks of hard work on your part is this: You will not get your dog to do anything until he respects you."

When the monologue wound down he grabbed a tin can from within a washtub near the wall behind him.

"Now, we are going to test the cognitive skills of your dogs so that we have an idea of how much to expect from them."

He took a small chunk of hotdog from a plate hidden from site in the tub. As he did so, Jake sniffed the air and his ears pricked forward, his body quivering a little. Rob had picked his favorite treat.

He put the hotdog under the can in the middle of the room and glanced at Jake.

"Each dog will be allowed a go at the can to figure out how to access the food. The smartest dogs will knock over the can in 5 seconds or less, others will take longer. One or two will not be able to figure it out and will either look at their human for help, or walk away." His gaze swept the room and lighted on Jake again. He crooked a finger at us like a claw. "Drop the leash."

He didn't seem to notice my poised cell phone. I had already decided to record his interaction with Jake in case I needed more evidence for Shannon to cancel the training. When he called, Jake hesitated, unwilling to go near him but so badly wanting the hotdog. He whined. I gave him a pat to encourage him and said "Go!" That was enough. He shot forward, past the test object, onto the table and into the washtub where he gobbled up the contents before an astonished audience.

Frowning, Rob tried to take hold of Jake's leash but the dog jumped out of the tub, knocking over the can with his nose and licking up the morsel so quick I almost didn't see it. He grinned at me with tail waving high.

Everyone clapped except Rob.

My phone still in hand, I grabbed his leash. The atmosphere seemed brighter to me as the foul odor receded. Rob's scowl didn't bother me much either.

"Were you recording that?" he asked. "No recordings allowed. Erase it, please."

"It's for my own personal use."

His expression turned mean as he strode toward me. "My training method is my livelihood and I don't want it on the Internet."

He grabbed for the phone. I wasn't prepared for the big grey ball of fury and teeth that hurdled between us, but with astonishing speed Rob jumped aside and Jake's jaws closed on air millimetres from his hand. One of the other students shrieked and several dogs barked. I dropped the phone and dove for Jake's leash with both hands. I managed to hold onto him as he barred his formidable teeth in Rob's direction.

Silence dropped over the room and I could almost hear my heart pounding. Rob held up his hand and examined it. His narrowed eyes met mine.

"I...I guess he thought you were going to hit me," I offered.

He appeared satisfied rather than angry. "He could have shredded the sinew and left me disabled. Your dog may have to be put down if we can't fix this behavior."

The pronouncement cut me like a knife. "No. I'll keep him at home."

"You do that. Take him out now and I'll call you later."

Without looking at anyone, I retrieved my phone and shoved it in my pocket before leading Jake from the building.

Chapter 7

We sat on the curb in front of the training center, Jake's leash wound securely around my hand. He pressed against me as if he thought I still needed protection. I kept playing the attack over and over in my mind trying to understand it. One thing for sure, if Rob hadn't been so agile, Jake would have injured him and gotten himself in serious trouble. But I'd never seen a person move so fast before.

Jake licked my hand, perhaps sensing my worry. I did not want to tell Shannon about his behavior given their history. This past Sunday afternoon things had gone from bad to worse when I tried to show her the commands Jake learned. He did well at first, but as soon as she clapped her approval, Jake jumped on her almost knocking her down.

Red-faced she wagged her finger at me. "You and Tony managed to teach him a couple of easy tricks but he still has no manners. Rob will show us how to get respect from the dog."

Communication between us had been cool since and she had dropped us off at the Alpha Guy center with a curt, "Don't screw this up."

I texted: "Jake tried to bite Rob. Come NOW"
Within seconds my phone played "Who Let The Dogs Out".
"Are you still in class?"
"ASAP." I hung up.
The session ended long before she showed up, the other students and their dogs spilling out from the building and skirting around us,

offering little waves or smiles from a safe distance as if we were contagious, while Jake's tail wagged a friendly greeting to all.

By the time Shannon's car pulled up to the curb Jake and I languished completely alone on the quiet street. She got out and held the back door open for Jake who was eager to duck out of the heat and plunged in without hesitation. I was not as fast, my attention overtaken by the way she looked.

"Your hair!"

Her head sported a neon orange orb of pixie short hair gel-spiked in a random mess. A sparkly pair of turquoise ornaments dangled from her earlobes.

The remodeling had taken place on other areas of her person as well. A layer of make up obliterated her freckles and a thick coat of red lipstick matched her hair. My eyes slid down to her bigger-than-usual chest in a tight fitted t-shirt and then barely-there blue shorts above her pale legs.

"What happened?" she snapped.

"Uhhh..."

"Okay, I've had a makeover, and you've stared long enough. Let's move on. Tell me why you didn't finish the class and it had better be good because I swear, Raine, your dog is this far from going to the animal shelter."

"Your hair is blinding me."

"Beige no more," she said. "What happened with Rob?"

"Your boobs are so big."

"Raine!"

From inside the car Jake barked and pawed at the window, snapping me out of my distraction. He needed to get out of the car.

"He almost bit Rob and I'm sorry but Rob provoked him, Shannon. Jake's never acted like that with anyone before."

"Well, he's lived with us less than four weeks so we don't really know him, do we? I need to find out what Rob plans to do," she said. "Is he still here?"

"I don't know, he said he would call you later. Let's just go home."

"Is he all right?"

Jake yelped inside the hot vehicle and continued to paw at the door until he accidentally pawed the lock button and it clicked open. I dived for the handle to release him and pulled him close before he jumped on Shannon.

"Ooo that dog is impossible. I've got to talk to Rob."

She hustled inside, leaving us in the shade of the building for almost 30 minutes. I started to wonder if something had happened to her when she finally re-emerged with a big dreamy, red-lipped smile.

We got into the car, and I rolled down Jake's window. He stuck his head out and gave a "good riddance" bark as we drove away.

Chapter 8

Shannon hummed a little tune and tapped her orange and yellow gel nails on the steering wheel.

I cleared my throat. "So what is Rob going to do?"

"Nothing. He says this isn't his first dangerous dog. Part of the job."

Relief. "Yes, I suppose business would suffer if he got upset every time."

Shannon flicked a glance my way. "He offered to come to our house for private lessons."

"What?! Why? He can't handle Jake."

"He says he can, in a closed setting without other dogs distracting the student. As long as we put a muzzle on the dog."

"No way."

"You don't want Rob to suffer a bite for real, do you?"

I fumed. "Boy, that guy is wily. I don't know what his game is, but he is up to something. Wily Wolf. He was the person in the orchard the other night, I'm sure of it now – he's interested in something at our house."

"Because you have it in for him, you are not thinking straight. He is trying to be nice in spite of your attitude."

"He should give us our money back so we can find a different trainer, one who can get along with our dog."

She pursed her lips. "You brought home a bad dog. If you don't let Rob help us, Jake can't continue to live here."

I tried to reason with her but she closed her mind and started humming again. Bobbing her chin, her orange hair gleaming, she resembled a brightly painted bobble head.

"What's with the sudden extreme make over?"

She smiled and stopped drumming. "Aren't you the one who is always pointing out how dull my life is? Well, say hello to colorful me."

She had never before taken such care with her appearance. The makeup and clothes enhanced her skin and figure, however the hair contradicted her normal personality - loud and fun.

"The outfit is a couple of sizes smaller than you usually buy which is a good thing, I guess." I paused. "You have nice legs, but some spray tan would help."

She straightened, enjoying the compliment. "That's next."

Her posture drew my attention to the unfamiliar chest profile. "Did Rob notice your, uhm, new figure?"

Her smile widened. "He said he likes my hair."

"I'll bet."

When we got home she turned off the car but did not get out.

"I'm so happy we're getting personal help with Jake. It's going to work out, you'll see," she assured me. "You can't give up too soon."

I didn't want to erase the hopefulness on her face. "Sure."

Jake and I went looking for Tony and found him moving a fake owl out of a tree. "I think the birds are on to this one." He wiped it off. "Those magpies up there are just laughing at me." He set the owl down and gave the huge happy dog some pats.

"Jake tried to bite Rob today," I said.

He regarded the wagging tail with surprise. "This guy?"

When I told him what happened he wanted to see the recording but the battery on my phone was low. I promised to email the link to him so he could show his brother too.

"Nick came out today with a wildlife officer. He said those prints are definitely from a wolf. Not really a mystery since a few people in the city keep domesticated wolf hybrids. Owning one is frowned upon because they will kill livestock and can be aggressive toward dogs. They also need lots of exercise so maybe someone was being careful to walk his wolf-dog in the evening so as not to draw attention."

"Does Nick think that's what Rob was doing?"

"He thinks someone was out walking, yes."

"Endangering your sheep."

His expression was grim. "They're penned beside the barn at night. Sassy did bark but I'm sure she would have put up more of a fuss if the wolf had been near them."

His explanation for what I'd seen was plausible, so I decided to try and forget about Rob in the orchard and concentrate on my dog training problem. Still, the unease I felt remained.

Chapter 9

That night a howling long-toothed beast made an encore appearance while I slept. As before, I could not outrun him or scream for help, but I could wake up and when I did, Jake was barking outside on my parents' balcony. I hurried out with the binoculars but not even the rustle of bats from the colony in the rocks above the orchard disturbed the stillness. I shushed Jake and listened for an answering bark or howl. No crickets or frogs or rustling leaves, nothing louder than my beating heart, made a sound. However, Jake remained alert so I did too, for another 15 minutes before giving up.

"Come on, Bud. You're sleeping with me again tonight."

The next morning Shannon and I sat across from each other and slurped our cereal and milk. I didn't bother telling her about Jake's restlessness since she would have considered it as more bad behavior for which we needed the god-like trainer, Rob.

I left Jake in the back yard before proceeding out to look for new signs of wolf-dog walkers. What I found instead was something even more disturbing, a large fresh mound of dirt big enough to be the grave of a small animal. A large green beetle was burrowing into it and I thought about going back to the house for some gardening gloves before I touched anything.

"Raine!"

Tony approached carrying hedge trimmers. He must have been a few rows over when he saw me. A thrill of pleasure fluttered inside me.

When he reached me I told him about Jake's barking.

"One of the lambs is missing," he said. "She wasn't with the rest of the flock in the pen this morning and I've looked all over our farm, in every ditch, and the Coopers to the west of us. I checked the fence for holes. None. Anyway, the sheep were all in the pen last night and no way she could have escaped by herself. To make matters worse, Sassy didn't raise any alarm. I can't figure out why."

I knew he took his responsibilities seriously and it hurt his pride to be the one to have lost an animal.

"I wish Jake could talk," I said.

He told me Nick had studied the dirt around the pen and barn but was unable to discern anything unusual amidst the hoof prints. Tony hadn't called his father, but had reluctantly informed Aunt Althea.

"She has already gone into action with her incantations and potions. She's banished me from the kitchen so she can cook something in a big black pot on the stove. I'm not kidding – she's got a witch's cauldron."

I laughed. "What does she think happened to the lamb?"

"Guess."

I gestured toward the mound. "It wasn't here yesterday."

He knelt down to examine it. "A small tool was used to scoop the dirt. And someone used that fallen branch over there to cover the tracks. He knows about distinctive sole patterns."

He plunged his gloved hands into the mound and uncovered a piece of braided black hair or fur about four inches long, tied at both ends with string. He sniffed and grimaced.

I stepped closer to him and coughed when the strong scent reached my nostrils. "Essence of chicken farm. Possibly a love charm... Maybe Rob has fallen in love with Shannon and made a spell to make her fall in love with him."

Tony rolled his eyes. "Men don't do stuff like that."

"Rob is a very unusual person."

"Even if your theory is correct, how is this relevant to my missing lamb?"

"Animal sacrifice and this little magic amulet? A powerful potion." All the things I learned during my werewolf research came to mind. "Crazy people do go out under a full moon and sacrifice animals and perform rituals...it doesn't mean I think this stuff works; only that some people do."

"There was no full moon last night."

"One must be coming up. You need to show this to Althea."

"Why? She's just going to make us wear a garlic necklace, or something equally kooky."

"Whoever did this probably operates in the same world she does. She can tell us what it means. Maybe this is a clue to the missing sheep."

We searched the rest of the area but uncovered nothing more and he conceded his aunt might be able to explain the mystery.

We found her reading a book under the umbrella beside the pool. Without even a "Hi, Auntie", Tony waved the fur under her nose.

"Look what somebody buried out in the orchard. Do you know what it could be for?"

She made a face and batted his hand away.

"What's wrong with you?" she asked but as her eyes focused on the object she dropped her book. Then her right hand darted around, writing in the air. She ended by making the sign of the cross and spitting to her right side three times. Afterward, she reached for her glass on the table and took a big refueling gulp. She sighed and spoke in Greek.

I was fascinated. Tony scowled.

"What did she do?" I asked.

"Warded off evil."

She pointed a trembling finger at us. "Wickedness waits for you..."

Tony turned his face so that only I could see him mouth the words, "I told you."

She cocked her head and looked into the distance, as if expecting the wickedness to swoop down at any moment.

"Wolfen." She curled her upper lip and spat the word like it tasted rotten on her tongue. "The wolfen buried a piece of its fur, soaked with its own urine, to call to its chosen mate. He will be here soon to collect. I warned you about this."

"Eew..." Tony dropped the fur.

I shivered in spite of the heat. She was as good as any movie witches. "Did the wolfen take the lamb too?"

"What do you think?"

"Interesting. I didn't know werewolves ate sheep," Tony said.

"They have to live," she insisted, her eyes unblinking. "So many places for a beast to hide."

"The only beasts up there are bats, Auntie."

"You know nothing," she snapped. "The spirit of the wolf lurks about waiting for the person who invited it." She narrowed her eyes at me with suspicion.

"You think the man I saw in the orchard was a werewolf?" I tried not to think of Rob but he was already in my head with his pointy nose, yellow eyes, and large teeth – which grew larger in my memory.

She considered my question. "We need more information to know for sure."

"We?" I said.

"My colleagues."

"Witch friends," Tony explained.

She frowned and wagged her finger. "No witches. *Professionals* from old country who know these things."

Tony's expression did not change. "How do you communicate? Magic steam from your cauldron?"

"Video chat, you smart mouth."

"Okay. Now stop putting ideas in Raine's head. We just wanted to ask you if this piece of buried fur had any significance."

"And I told you. Did you put the bags under your pillows?" she asked me.

"Yes." I avoided looking at Tony and thinking of Shannon's unreasonable attraction to Rob I asked, "Do werewolves have a mysterious power over their victims?"

Tony swore under his breath as Althea matter-of-factly informed me: "You need more protection." She hoisted herself out of the chair and went back into the house.

"Now you're going to be awarded a hundred more of those smelly bags," he said, dipping his hands in the pool to wash them. I sat at the edge of the pool and cooled my feet.

He made a sour face. "I hope she at least cooked something good for supper. She's so obsessed with her potions."

She soon returned carrying an old black book held together with twine and handed it to me. The title, *Secrets of The Wolfen* was etched in a gothic font surrounding a white sketch of a snarling wolf's head on a human body. The eyes of the beast glowed amber.

She looked about as if spirits might be listening and explained in a low voice she was called to protect us.

"Years ago I found this book on a bench near Vatican City. It was meant for this time. Now I give it to you, as you have need of it."

"What?!" Tony said. "I didn't know you knew the Pope, Auntie."

"Italy is not far from Greece. And there is a lot you don't know about me, boy," she said.

I stroked the cover of the book and regarded the scary eyes of the beast, ready to leap out and devour me.

Aunt Althea drew another sign in the air. "The creature prowls the land. You and your sister are unprotected lambs while your parents are away..."

"Please stop trying to scare my friend," Tony said.

She frowned at him. "Life isn't always safe. You need to accept that before it is too late." She picked the fur off the cement. "I will burn this. It weakens the power." She went back inside.

He scowled.

"What does Nick say about her beliefs?" I asked.

"He's amused."

I looked out toward the peaceful pasture rising up to the hills, our picture perfect refuge. It was hard to imagine anything evil out here, especially something like a mythical werewolf. But Althea was so persuasive. Whatever the thing was she believed in, it was certainly real to her and deserved some investigation.

Tony wasn't convinced at all. "I don't even believe she was ever at the Vatican. You should leave that book here."

He tried to take it but I moved away. "Do you think your own aunt is lying?"

"She isn't operating in the real world."

"What world is she operating in, Tony?"

"Whatever it is, we should avoid it," he said.

"If we ignore everything she has said, what other explanation is there for the man in the orchard one night, a missing lamb and buried token the next?"

"Homeless man with mental health issues or maybe somebody's pet wolf got out and he was trying to recapture it without getting into trouble. Or two unrelated situations that coincidentally occurred around the same time."

I thought Aunt Althea's theories were as likely as Tony's.

Chapter 10

J ake followed me to my room and flopped down on the floor while I
sprawled on the bed to study *Secrets of the Wolfen*. The pages were
soft and supple like cloth and held together with thin leather ties. I'd
never seen anything like it.

Handwritten calligraphy-style text in indigo ink flowed from page
to page, with drawings of werewolves, plants and terrified maidens in
the margins.

Aunt Althea had given me an artifact of secret knowledge and it
thrilled me to my core.

Tony thought his old aunt was either crazy or making things up.
I, however, believed that outside of my own experiences many
possibilities existed. Althea had lived a long time. Who was I to dismiss
her beliefs?

After all, the Greeks were the first to figure out the earth is round
and not flat. These were Aunt Althea's ancestors, crazy people who
happened to be right.

Eagerly I studied the book. Even though I could accept Tony's
alternate explanations for the strange events of late, a little part of
me did not completely disregard the more interesting explanation of
shape-shifting animals lurking in the orchard. My own theory began to
form, that unexplained supernatural creatures prowled at the edges of
civilization – not God's creatures, but hybrids of evil.

"You know, don't you Jake? What do you see?"

He thumped his tail from where he lay chewing on one of Shannon's running shoes, already beyond repair from previous attacks. The hidden wolf-repellant bag did not bother him so one thing was for sure – they didn't work on dogs.

The first chapter of *Secrets* reported actual werewolf sightings. However, since it was an old book they had long entered into the realm of legend rather than credible history. For more recent stories I searched the Internet and found the well-documented sightings of a wolf-like beast in Southern Wisconsin. Referred to as the Beast of Bray Road, many people had seen it and many more were searching for it.

This was not fiction, but actual eye-witness accounts of frightening encounters on dark and lonely roads with an unusual wolf-like animal that walked upright like a man. I got goose bumps reading about them. The sightings occurred in a farming area, like ours, and I wondered how many times the Wisconsin beast stood and stared up into the lighted windows of isolated farm homes looking for a mate, while innocent sisters waited for their parents to come home?

I shuddered. No recent encounters had been recorded in that area so the logical question was, why not? Did he die? Or MAYBE the beast had migrated to our part of the continent.

I considered the possibility that if werewolves existed, Rob could be one. It made perfect sense: He was the only guy who had been around our place besides Tony, and I was sure it had been him in our orchard the night after we registered for dog training.

The book contained a section on how to identify a werewolf in human form, including a checklist of the most obvious traits. I studied the information, tracing the calligraphy with my fingers, feeling the connection to the supernatural there. I conjured an image of Rob at the Alpha Guy Center:

1. long canine teeth – CHECK
2. dark thick hair - CHECK

3. Yellow eyes – CHECK
4. excellent hearing – CHECK
5. paleness - CHECK
6. bizarre behavior – DOUBLE CHECK
7. aggressive toward other canines - CHECK

The rest I had yet to confirm:

1. excellent sense of smell
2. curved thumbnail
3. long middle fingers
4. hairy palms
5. enjoys chasing small animals such as rabbits and cats
6. unprovoked rages
7. insomnia
8. restlessness
9. dry eyes
10. an unnatural dread of open water
11. long tongue
12. always thirsty (more observation needed).

The book said that although werewolves are seen mainly at night, they do not need a full moon to shape shift. This myth is rooted in dramatic fiction and Hollywood.

Just putting it all down on paper helped me feel a little more in control. I planned to test him for the other 12 traits, sure that if I could document with my camera, a few of them, Shannon and Tony would start to believe me. Or at least entertain the possibility and stop thinking I was crazy.

When Jake and I went down to the kitchen the next morning Shannon was sitting at the island in trendy pink sweat pants, a bran muffin in front of her while she chattered on her phone. She turned away from me and lowered her voice, "She's here. Talk to you later." And clicked off.

"Who were you talking to?" I found a chew bone in the cupboard behind her and tossed it to Jake. He caught it with a rather proud flourish.

"What a good clever boy you are, Jakey-Wakey," I said in my doggie talk voice.

Shannon snorted.

I took an apple out of the fridge and repeated my question.

She made a face at Jake who gnawed on the bone with great enthusiasm. "I hate that slobbering noise."

I was not about to let her get away with ignoring me. "For the third time, who were you talking to on your phone?"

"My business."

"No need to be so cagey. I know it was Rob."

"Then why did you ask?"

"What were you talking about?"

She avoided meeting my eyes. "Uh, I had to phone him to clarify some things regarding the training. How involved I needed to be...that sort of thing."

I bit into my apple and made loud smacking noises. "You should phone him back and complain about Jake's slobbering."

She threw a scowl. I finished my apple and Jake continued to smack on his chew.

"Are you going to try to be normal when he gets here this afternoon? Or are you going to torment him?"

I tossed the core into the garbage. "I'm not the expert on tormenting, Rob is. He's not nice, Shannon."

Her lips formed a thin line. "Don't you think it was pretty darn generous of him to offer to come here for one-on-one training? He told me he usually charges $50 an hour for house calls."

"Why is he granting YOU such a big favor?"

She pretended to be busy wiping off the counter.

"You think he likes you, don't you?" I said.

"What of it?" She met my eyes defiantly. "Don't you think a man could be interested in me?"

"I don't understand this at all. Genius science girl decides her first crush will be on a guy with mysterious canine traits...oh, I get it! He's your biology project, right?"

"You're such a riot, ha, ha. Canine traits. Ha ha. For your information, I think he is hot."

"There are other men," I pointed out. "Much nicer. And hotter."

A dreamy smile settled on her face. "Rob is not like all those immature guys I know. Something flowed between us when he shook my hand."

"Oh puleese. He has warm hands. Doesn't mean you're soul mates."

While she tried to think of a clever retort, I took the opportunity to tell her about Tony's missing lamb.

"Kind of mysterious, don't you think? A lamb goes missing soon after I see somebody sneaking around our property?"

She smiled. "Worrisome, but eliminates Rob as a suspect. What would he need a lamb for?"

"To eat?"

Her expression darkened. "Or maybe he knits and can't afford to buy some wool at the knit shop?"

"You know, I never thought of that. You and I should do more brainstorming."

"He's going to be here in a few hours. Grow up a little before then, please."

Chapter 11

Rob was due at 1 p.m. and Shannon started getting ready around 10 a.m. Apparently it took hours to be a natural beauty.

Just before his expected arrival, I stationed myself at the front window – standing back at the side so as not to be seen. At 12:59 a black SUV rolled up the driveway, settled in front of the house and discharged Rob. He loped up the steps and rang twice before I let him in.

He offered me a humorless smile. "Hi Raine. Are you and the dog ready for some work?"

Without waiting for an answer he strutted past me and studied the living room, the faint odor from the training center trailing him. If he felt my disapproval he gave no indication.

"I hope Shannon understood she should be joining us today. Family members must be involved when we are working with a difficult dog."

"Oh, she understood all right. She'll be down in a minute."

An awkward silence stretched out between us. He made no effort to thaw the atmosphere, which didn't surprise me. The soul of a wolf would not incline him to make small talk.

Idly he scratched his right palm, drawing my attention to a hair growing there before he turned the hand away and flexed his fingers. I also noticed his middle fingers were a little longer than normal, and his thumbnails were slightly curved, as well as too long. In addition his knuckles were rather hairy - not mentioned in the book, but kinda wolfish.

When I saw his left wrist, I couldn't stop my quick intake of breath.

"What are you looking at?" he demanded.

"I, ah, am just admiring your watchband. Is that animal fur?"

A wide braid of black fur, similar in style to the piece we found buried in the orchard, encircled his wrist. Inwardly horrified, I think I did a pretty good job of appearing cool.

He stroked the band with his thumb. "Dog fur, a trainer's charm."

"Where would you get something like that?"

"I got it as a gift from a grateful client." He made no effort to keep the irritation out of his voice

"You weren't wearing it at the training center," I said.

"What difference does it make?"

This was more than a coincidence. I needed another consultation with Aunt Althea. Soon.

Shannon chose that moment to make her grand entrance from upstairs. She had settled on a plain white sundress with thin straps and a bright orange belt – similar to the shade of her hair - cinched at her waist. Gold sandals made the perfect setting for her red manicured toenails, and her hair had been coaxed into a sleek pixie do.

My outfit – up swept ponytail, white tennis shoes, khaki shorts and a fitted lime green shirt – seemed shabby in comparison. Alpha Guy stared at Shannon and licked his lips. I noted that he did that a lot but too fast for whipping out my smart phone and taking a picture. I pulled the phone from my pocket to be ready next time. Meanwhile, my sister dimpled and gushed like a school girl.

"Welcome to our home, Rob," she said.

"I was hoping you'd be here," he replied.

The sappy moment drew a fake cough from me irritating both of them.

"Are you ready to start?" Rob said sharply. "Since you mentioned in class that you saw an intruder in your orchard the other night I thought I should also test Jake's aptitude for guarding."

Shannon spoke quickly. "I don't want to make a big thing out of our so-called intruder. My sister is a little high strung right now - I think she misses our parents."

He said he understood our anxiety at being alone at night surrounded by hills and trees. He touched her lightly on the wrist as he spoke and the expression on her face made me afraid she might go into spasms.

"We're not really by ourselves," I said. "Mr. Abel, Dad's friend, pops in at all hours of the day to check on us, and of course our neighbors on both sides are keeping an eye out for us."

"What did Mr. Abel say about the intruder?" Rob asked, concern dripping from his voice.

"He says he is going to put up security cameras."

Shannon gave me a look but she couldn't be sure what I may have discussed with Mr. Abel, which was good, since I hadn't seen him. He was a busy farmer whose wife was 8 1/2 months pregnant with their first child. His phone number beside our phone was the extent of his input. I hoped helpful Shannon would not have an occasion to tell this to Rob.

Rob accepted my information and reassured her that she could call him the next time something unusual happened and he would come with his protection dog.

I knew she was not worried about danger since more important things, like her appearance to members of the opposite sex, occupied her mind. Only a few days ago this had been her top reason to dismiss my friends and me as "shallow". Witnessing her performance, I could now understand her disgust.

"Okay, let's get to work, shall we?" He rubbed his palms together and I tried again to spot – unsuccessfully – any hair on them.

Shannon pointed through the kitchen toward the back and Rob led the way as if he owned the place.

As he approached the water cooler next to the sliding doors I offered him a drink. He accepted and Shannon hustled to bring him one. He drank with a little slurping sound and licked his lips with his long tongue.

He helped himself to another full glass and took it with him when he stepped out onto the deck. Having seen him approach, Jake stood with rigid legs, tail high, and erupted with a string of sharp barks. I don't speak dog but I know what "Go away!" sounds like.

I clipped on his leash and silently prayed that Rob would go easy this time. He handed his drained glass to Shannon and put his hands on his hips.

"He is supposed to be muzzled for this session." He caught sight of the muzzle Shannon bought hanging on a hook by the door and seized it. "Put this on him, now."

I didn't know what to do. I didn't want Jake to be without protection.

"Raine," Shannon warned, "Rob already has a good reason to report him as a dangerous animal."

I took the muzzle and slowly slipped it over Jake's head. He stood stiff, allowing me to do so, but the reproach in his body language almost made me cry. I stroked his head and whispered an apology.

To Rob I coldly explained that Jake already knew basic commands. He shrugged. "Those are easy. What you two ladies want is a dog with manners. Behavior training is my specialty."

He reached for Jake's collar, but Jake lunged for the hand, his jaws snapping inside the muzzle. Rob reflexively pulled back and Jake took the opportunity to get away, jumping past him through the doorway and kitchen, and up the stairs.

I chased him all the way to my room where he slid on his belly under my desk, knocking over the chair.

Chapter 12

Following close behind me Rob stopped short at the doorway, his face twisting in disgust.

"Do you have a rotting corpse in here?"

Shannon pushed past him into the room. Her nose wrinkled. "Ugh. I think I smelled it last night in my room, too." She eyed me with suspicion and I gave a little shrug while inwardly I celebrated. Aunt Althea's pillow potion worked! I must have grown used to the odor, having slept with it for three nights, but Rob's reaction was extreme.

"Why don't you come in here for Jake?" I said. "I'm having trouble."

He put his hand over his nose, the fur watchband drawing my attention like a hypnotist's watch. He turned away. "I think I'm going to vomit. Bring your dog outside." He left.

"What IS that stink, Raine?" Shannon surveyed the room.

"Uh, maybe my running shoes." I made a mental note to double wrap the bag.

"You should throw them away. And check your room for fecal matter."

"Rob must be hyper sensitive."

"Get the dog outside. Now."

"Don't you see he is doing the opposite of what we hired him to do? He is about to mess up my dog."

"Stop whining now. His classes are always full for a reason. If you don't come back he will think you are a crybaby." She left.

Having witnessed his inability to cross the threshold into my bedroom I was less concerned about being a crybaby and more concerned about being prey. I couldn't tell Shannon this. Not until I had more proof.

I managed to coax Jake out from under the desk and downstairs, bribing him with pieces of hot dog, for which I had to take off the muzzle. Once outside, I heard Shannon laughing like a girly girl at something Rob said. They stood too close together on my parent's balcony admiring the view, but when they noticed Jake and me they moved apart and joined us on the lower level.

Rob motioned toward the Callas property. "Once Jake gets the idea to go after those sheep next door he won't have trouble clearing the fence. If he hasn't already."

As I repositioned the muzzle I assured him that Jake had never shown any interest in the sheep.

"You can't really be sure what he does at night, can you?" He sniffed the air in a peculiar manner as if something had wafted our way. "He knows those sheep are there. We should test him. You go on the other side and call his name."

I stayed put. "You want to teach him to jump the fence?"

He looked to Shannon for back up but she remained silent, perhaps wondering the same thing. "Okay forget it. Let's get back to training."

I felt confident since we had been practicing at home. With Rob and Shannon standing a few feet away, I maneuvered Jake into a 'sit' in front of me. Although he understood we were playing the 'yes' game and was happy about that, his guard was still up.

I said his name and motioned him to drop down onto his belly. He did beautifully, keeping his eyes on me. I held up my hand and backed away. He knew what I expected of him and stayed put. When I was even with Rob and Shannon I stopped and waited, hoping Jake would too.

"Not bad," Rob said.

Shannon agreed, whether for my sake or Rob's, I don't know. I wanted to keep Jake in a "stay" for at least five minutes, and so far he held, his attention fixed on me, ears forward. Then Rob decided to charge Jake, yelling and flapping his arms. The dog immediately leaped up, barking aggressively inside the muzzle. I took hold of the leash.

"What are you doing?" I demanded.

He smirked. "He's not well-trained yet, is he? He is still far too reactive to be trusted. How did you train him?"

I told him about positive conditioning to which he shook his head. "You're turning him into a spoiled brat who won't do anything without a reward."

"So? I don't mind rewarding him."

"No. This strong-willed dog requires a pack leader. I'll show you." He whisked the leash out of my hand. He yanked savagely straight up until Jake's front paws came off the ground and he was forced to sit back on his haunches. When Rob let up on the tension Jake stood up, so Rob yanked again, his yellow eyes bright with satisfaction.

Jake squirmed and growled and tried to get away and I just stood there, feeling like a horrible dog betrayer. Shannon turned her head away.

Rob darted out of reach when I attempted again to take the leash, while Jake tried desperately to remove the muzzle with his paw.

"Enough!" I yelled.

This time he allowed me to take it. "You're going to have to spend every spare moment working with him."

I shook with anger and avoided looking at him while I stroked my dog.

He must have realized it was pointless to continue. "I'll see you in a couple of days," he said to Shannon. She walked him to the back gate where they talked for a moment.

I removed the muzzle and scratched Jake's neck and listened but they spoke too quietly for me to catch what they said. After he was gone Shannon returned to the kitchen for a bottle of water from the fridge.

"Well?" I said.

She took a long drink from the bottle.

"Did you not see the same abuse I saw?"

She furrowed her brow and thought. "I admit it looked harsh. But if that's what it takes to get results..."

I snapped. "What's wrong with you? Are you so hypnotized by him that you can't be rational?"

"No. You are indulging in anthropomorphism where Jake is concerned."

"Anthrop...what?"

"Humanizing your dog. Jake is not your little brother, Raine. To us Rob's behavior may look like abuse, but to Jake it is the authority he respects. Rob explained it all to me."

"Uh huh. Well, I refuse to treat Jake like Rob did and I do not want him here anymore." I folded my arms. "I don't care about the money, I forfeit my share. I'll even pay you back for your half."

She tried to stare me down but I was determined and she knew I was through. "Rob could issue a complaint against Jake with the city."

"I'll fight for Jake. Nick will help me. You should be sticking up for us too."

She looked away.

I was so frustrated. "Rob is here to sniff around you." Then I did what I considered a good imitation of his constant sniffing. Sniff, sniff, sniff.

Jake seemed to enjoy the entertainment and wagged his tail - the whole previous episode forgotten. Out of sight, out of mind, a great dog trait.

"See, he doesn't look traumatized to me. In fact, he's considerably calmer than usual. Rob is having a positive effect whether you like him or not. Just give him one more chance. If you still think his methods don't work I will concede and we can hire another trainer."

"Why one more time, Shannon? So you can see him again?"

"What's wrong with that?"

"You can do better than him," I said.

"Just because you don't agree with his dog training methods you believe he is also a bad human?"

"No. There's something about him...like he's not stable."

"That's so judgmental."

"Yes, it is. In a discerning kind of way."

Too bad one of the first guys who caught her interest was crazy at best, a werewolf at worst. Then I realized I needed to see him again to try to determine for certain his nature – human or beast - and why he was so interested in Jake and Shannon.

"Tell him no more jerking Jake's leash," I said.

Chapter 13

Another werewolf ambushed my dreams that night and I woke up with a little yelp and Jake's wet nose pushing into my hand. Surprisingly, the dog snot comforted me, something real but easily washed off and forgotten.

I couldn't sleep anymore so I turned on my light and got out *Secrets of the Wolfen* to go back over a few things.

According to the book, while in the shape of a man the werewolf searches for the perfect human female. Once he finds her, he waits until a full moon to bite her. This wound festers over a period of 30 days until she shifts into his lupus mate.

Rob wanted my sister, beast or not, and bad news either way. Shannon was like an innocent baby bird trying to fly, and he was ready to eat her. As annoyed as I was with Shannon, I didn't want her to get into trouble with either a werewolf or a human jerk. I needed to convince her of the danger by using evidence regarding Rob's species that she couldn't deny. If the tests proved he was something less than human, I would move on to studying – and applying - *Methods of Elimination, Chapter 6.*

I fell asleep reading and woke up the next day with barely enough time to get to work. As soon as Jake and I got home that afternoon, we headed over to the Callas' house. I didn't text Tony, hoping to be able to talk to his aunt alone.

Aunt Althea surprised me coming down from the direction of the hill on the other side of the fence separating our properties. A wide-brimmed straw hat shaded her face and she carried a large linen bag bulging with long-stemmed lupine flowers, their pink and purple heads peeking out over the top.

After a short greeting, she said, "The wolf man haunts you."

I was relieved to unburden myself on someone who didn't dismiss me as an over imaginative person. I related the previous day's training session with Rob including his wolf characteristics, and she listened calmly until I mentioned the fur watchband.

She spat out something in Greek and made her air sign.

This time her behavior didn't seem so crazy to me. I described my latest dream. "I know Tony doesn't believe this but I think there is a connection between Rob in the orchard and the missing lamb. Maybe my dream is a warning."

She started walking and I fell into step beside her. "Some men require a bite in the...in order to believe." She pointed to her generous behind and let out a witchy cackle. "Your werewolves – are they large black beasts with blood on their teeth?"

She knew! I shivered and scanned the bright green countryside for wolfen hiding places.

A rabbit taking off from it's hiding place a few feet away startled us and Jake took off after it. Althea watched them disappear behind a storage shed and whispered, "If the wolfen was near, the dog would know."

She was right. Jake always reacted to Rob. I relaxed. From now on, I would keep him near at all times.

"You have a gift. Come, we will talk more." We proceeded to Tony's house.

Once inside, she motioned for me to sit in the breakfast nook. She cut and arranged the flowers in two large vases while I described Rob's and Shannon's mutual attraction. She nodded in an inscrutable way, and occasionally made her air drawings.

"What should I do next?"

Her dark eyes assessed me. "There are ways to test the man for the sign of the wolf."

I leaned forward. "The book you gave me has a whole chapter on that. Are those the methods you use?"

"I must think." She took two bottles of water out of the fridge and put one in front of me. Then she got a glass for herself and poured from her bottle.

The front door opened with a loud crack. Tony, dusty and sweaty, tromped in.

"What are you doing here?"

"Hello Tony," I said.

"Milk and sandwiches in the refrigerator," Aunt Althea said.

He smiled but I sensed he wasn't comfortable with my solo visit with Althea. He went to the refrigerator, pulled out a carton of milk and took a long draw from it while Althea clucked disapprovingly. With his thirst eased, he leaned against the counter.

"How was the lesson?"

"Rob wears a watchband made of black fur."

His eyes widened and I repeated what I'd told Althea.

"Young girls love wolfen," Althea added. "The creature put a spell on her sister."

He laughed. "The ultimate bad boy. Us nice guys don't stand a chance."

I didn't like the mockery. "You are not a nice guy."

He feigned an expression of hurt. "Come on. Who drove you to meet your friends at the beach a couple of weeks ago?"

"Don't you think the fur watchband is more than a coincidence? He was out in the orchard."

"SOMEONE was in your orchard. AND lots of people have lots of different watchbands, so nothing really connects here." He got his sandwiches out of the fridge and added, "I can't believe I'm participating in this conversation."

After he sat down with his lunch he asked his aunt, "Have you ever seen a wolfen?"

She stabbed a finger in his direction. "Very few people who see a werewolf survive to report the experience. When I was a child, a young woman disappeared from our village the night before she was to be married. There was a mark on the floor beside her bed, three scratches beside each other, like a claw. I didn't see the beast but I saw the mark."

I swallowed. "There is a mark?"

"Not surprising," Tony said. "Okay, let's pretend for a minute werewolves really exist – Which They Don't – why are you so determined that Rob is one?"

I didn't want Tony to think I was crazy and as I mentally ran down the list I knew my evidence was weak. Nevertheless I tried: "He was repelled from entering my room because of that bag your aunt gave me...and..."

He laughed rudely. "I can guarantee, most males are repelled by the smell of rotting corpses, especially in a girl's bedroom."

"Let me finish. He's always sniffing, like a bloodhound."

"He has sinus problems."

"His eyes are yellow – like a wolf's."

"So? My eyes are brown, like a bear."

Aunt Althea decided to help. "The fur bracelet connects him to the animal spirit." She paused dramatically. "The wolf needs the man to call to the girl."

Tony put up a hand. "Can we talk about something else until I go back to work, please?"

"Any more ideas on finding your missing lamb?" I asked.

He shook his head. "I'm sure some sort of predator got it."

Aunt Althea gave him a knowing look. He shook his head and snorted. "It somehow escaped the pen and something got it." He stood up. "I don't like having to defend a reasonable explanation against make believe."

He left. I watched through the window as he headed for the barn and wondered if he was right. After all, I had been focusing on things that could make Rob a werewolf, and not on things that couldn't.

After a moment the old lady pointed to the flowers she had collected.

"Wolfsbane," she said.

I studied them. There was a reference to wolfsbane with an illustration in *Secrets of the Wolfen* – it was a flower used throughout the centuries to repel or poison wolves and toxic to humans as well. The name sounded much more sinister than these flowers looked.

"If he is a wolfen when he catches the scent his teeth will grow big and sharp, and he will foam at the mouth giving you time to run away."

"Are you sure they're not lupine?"

"Doesn't matter. The wolfen thinks it is wolfsbane and will avoid it."

She sensed I was still skeptical and chose her words. "It depends on what kind of werewolf he is. If he is the devil's spawn, a man merely bitten by a wolfen, it will work. However, if he is a werewolf because of his own spell, it might not. In that case you need a cat."

The book had also detailed the two different kinds of werewolves, the devil-made beast being harder to eliminate. But cats had not been mentioned.

"What kind do you think our werewolf is?"

"Self-made. It could even be someone from around here who made a deal with the devil for worldly powers."

"Rob." I said.

She nodded knowingly. "He wants power in the world of canines but now the beast controls him, he does not control the wolf."

"So why do I need a cat?"

"Ancient enemy. Tony can bring one from the barn over to your house."

"He will think it's a stupid idea."

"Nevertheless, he will do what you ask."

"He will? Did you put a spell on him?"

She laughed. "No. You did."

I knew what she meant but I knew she was probably wrong about that. Something else worried me: "What if the test proves Rob is a werewolf? What then?"

"Come talk to me and we will make a plan. Okay?"

"If I live."

"You should be okay."

I left the house carrying a bouquet of purple lupine and white daisies in a grocery bag. Sheep bleated in the barn accompanied by Tony's low voice comforting them. I wanted to talk to him again but I hesitated, not sure I would be welcomed when he was working. I went a few feet past the door just before it slid open.

"On your way home?

A black and white cat exited the barn and flopped in the dust at my feet, so I bent down to stroke it. "I need to borrow a cat. I saw a mouse in the kitchen yesterday and so far it has avoided the trap I put out."

"Why haven't you mentioned a mouse problem before?"

"If you bring the cat over tomorrow you will be able to meet Rob and see for yourself what I've been talking about."

"Sure, Rainy. I guess it couldn't hurt to meet him. Maybe I'll learn some dog training tips myself."

Aunt Althea was right, he didn't want to say no to me. "Thanks," I said, and had an insane impulse to give him a quick hug. But I didn't. Instead I let another awkward silence stretch out.

"Sure. I've got to get back to work now," he said.

As I walked home, I wondered what was going on between Tony and me now. Had Althea put a spell on us?

Chapter 14

Rob's next visit came too soon for me, but not for Shannon - she even managed to shorten her class at the science camp center and got home an hour before his arrival so she could practice the ancient female ritual of continuous costume change. She was faster this time though, and waited at the door in another new outfit, hair messy and spiked, when the doorbell rang.

"Oh Rob," she said, with a breathless voice.

Rob winked at her and even bestowed a cheerful smile on me. He still wore the wolf-band, I assumed to enhance the spell he had over Shannon.

This time she led the way to the back with me trailing behind Rob. The bouquet from Althea rested on the kitchen island beside the sink. He paid no attention to them so I hurried around the table to block him and picked up the vase. Tipping the flowers toward him, I smiled. "Aren't these beautiful?"

Startled, he stepped back. His brows twitched then his face collapsed into a sneeze. He shook his head, as if to rid himself of another loud wet noise, and his mouth exploded. He staggered a little as he sneezed again and again.

Rob's eyelids swelled up into red slits while Shannon and I gawked. I hadn't expected the fake wolfsbane to work so well.

"Get those flowers out of here," he bellowed between sneezes. Tears ran from his eyes and down his chin.

I affected a sympathetic tone, and stepped forward when he moved back. "Oh no. Are you allergic to them?"

Shannon plucked a tea towel from a drawer. She pressed it into his hand to dab at the wet stuff flowing from his facial orifices, including the wolf-like drool. I made a mental note to put that towel in the trash, if he ever finished wiping his nose.

Would an actual werewolf be so concerned about personal slobber, especially if he was gearing up to run away?

I moved closer to him with the flowers. Rob jerked back and erupted in another coughing fit.

"You ninny," Shannon said and snatched the vase out of my hands. She scurried out the back door and slammed the flowers into the trash bin. In the meantime, Rob kept his mouth and nose buried in the towel. His yellow eyes above the rim of the pretty floral cloth fixed on me, and not in a nice way.

Shannon returned. "Would an antihistamine help?"

He nodded mutely.

She scurried about until she found the medicine and a glass of water, and anxiously followed his movements as he downed the pill. I was impressed with her ability to stand so close to a person oozing stuff.

"Gosh, you are allergic," I said. "The severity of your reaction is almost inhuman, one might say."

"I am allergic to lupine." His voice was growly but it could have been from his coughing fit. As yet his large teeth were the same, without extra saliva escaping his mouth.

Unusual for a guy to be able to name lupine, I thought. "Interesting. What other plants are you allergic to? Monkshood?"

His eyes narrowed with suspicion. "Monkshood was used to kill wolves in years gone by, a barbaric practice that eliminated thousands of those noble creatures. The plant is poison. Why do you ask?"

"Just curious."

"Nutsy and clueless, is more like it," Shannon said. "Rob, do you want to rest for a while? Coffee or tea?"

Loud, gross nasal sounds delayed his answer but eventually he said he wanted to get to work.

I admit, he behaved more like an allergic and annoyed human than a raging wolf man, and I was a bit disappointed. I planned to inform Althea that ordinary purple flowers don't work.

As soon as we entered the back yard Jake barked at Rob. I tried to calm him down with a piece of hot dog I had snuck into my pocket. Rob forbade treats or "bribes" as he called them.

Jake was not too stressed to be distracted by his favorite food and he wagged his tail a little after he licked it up. Rob noticed the exchange and pounced, bellowing like a drill sergeant. "No treats! Do you want your dog to completely disrespect you?"

Of course, Jake started barking again and Shannon thought she would help by yelling at the dog. All I could do was hold onto his collar.

Time to bring in the cat.

I instructed Tony to arrive a few minutes after Rob was due and he did not let me down. Rob ordered me to put the muzzle and leash on Jake just as the gate rattled and Tony called "Hello."

He entered with a pet carrier and I flashed a big smile since I'd never been so glad to see anyone in my life.

"Everybody, Tony is here," I said unnecessarily.

Shannon frowned. "Nice of you to drop by. With a cat."

This was the first time he'd seen her since the makeover, and he had trouble tearing his eyes away, barely managing a "Hi" for Rob.

Jake greeted him with his usual love and slobber and Tony returned the attention. Rob gave him a measuring, unfriendly eye.

"What's with the cat?" Shannon asked.

Tony shot me an I-should-have-known look. "Raine said you have a mouse."

"I'm pretty sure I saw a mouse in the kitchen, Shannon," I said quickly and opened the carrier. Out strolled the black and white cat. She was calm and allowed me to pick her up for a cuddle.

"Would you like to pet her, Rob?"

He took the cat from me and sniffed. Then he wrinkled his nose like a prissy old woman. "Barn cat," he said with disdain.

He held her in front of Jake who quivered with excitement and gave a loud bark. The terrified feline scratched its way out of Rob's hold, drawing a pained yelp from him.

She tore her way through the yard with Jake so close behind she must have been able to feel the dog's breath up her butt. She clawed her way up the fence and took off on the other side. Before I could decide to go after her, Jake followed, scaling the 6-foot fence as if he did it every night.

I yelled "Jake!" and ran to the gate with Tony beside me and the other two behind. Once out in the yard we observed dog and cat head to the orchard. When the cat leapt into a tree Jake made a good effort to follow, but ended up bouncing back down to earth. He whined a little, circled and tried bouncing up again before giving up. He trotted to me with tail high, proud to have vanquished the new creature. Scaling the fence had been impressive but dangerous to know. I hooked the leash onto his collar and we returned to the back yard.

"BAD dog," Rob hollered, his hand over the claw marks on his right arm. I saw that the watchband caught Tony's eye as well.

I made sure Jake stayed out of Rob's reach. "He doesn't know he's not supposed to chase cats. We don't have any."

"He jumped that fence like it was nothing," Tony said with awe.

"We all saw the dog jump the fence," Rob said, his hands on his hips. "I warned you. I wonder if he has been hunting at night?" He gestured toward the sloping field where Tony's sheep were grazing.

Before I could retort Tony jumped in. "If he was hunting, we would have found a carcass or two around here, don't you think? Besides, he ignores the sheep when he's at our farm."

Rob didn't like Tony's interference. "Time for us to work, and let your friend retrieve his cat."

"We had better put something on those scratches," Shannon said, running her hand lightly over the bloody wounds. I wanted to stop her from touching him, but I knew my objection would infuriate her.

"Shannon, you should wash your hands," I managed, my voice quaking.

"Thanks for the tip," she said without a shred of sincerity. She cast a 'you're weird' look my way, but switched her expression to address Rob. "We can resume training after we've washed your wound."

"Good idea," Tony said and frowned at me. "Raine can help me get my cat out of the tree." He retrieved the pet carrier and stalked toward the orchard.

I was grateful to avoid a few minutes of Rob, but Tony wasn't happy with me either. However, I left Jake inside the yard and followed him. As soon as we reached the tree and its meowing resident, he faced me. "Explain the cat."

I couldn't meet his eyes. "Well, Aunt Althea said..."

He swore. Not good.

"Did you see the watch band?" I asked, trying to divert his attention.

He folded his arms, taking on a slightly uppity stance, which annoyed me. "Yes. It proves nothing. And - " He put up a hand to stop my protest. "- And, yes, he is not a warm guy. Listen, Raine, try to think this through. If all the things he does make him a werewolf, there are a lot of potential werewolves in the world, so you should gather more of Aunt Althea's rotting herb bags and stay in your room."

I folded my arms in imitation and we must have made an interesting picture mirroring each others' posture. "You think I'm nuts."

"No, but you do get focused on things and forget what's important. Like not using your friend."

I realized he was more hurt than angry and that got to me. I apologized.

He didn't respond.

"Won't you forgive me?" I said.

"I'll think about it," he said and the corners of his mouth lifted a little. For one insane moment I wanted to kiss him.

At that point the cat started climbing down on her own. Tony put her back into the carrying case.

"I'll see you later." He turned and headed through the orchard.

It bothered me a lot I had made Tony mad at me, so I was in no mood for dealing with Rob anymore that day and went right up to my room. Shannon didn't notice I was missing because she never came looking for me. After about 20 minutes I heard the front door close and a minute later, Rob's SUV started up and drove away.

Chapter 15

Later that evening, while I was re-reading the chapter on how to positively identify a werewolf, Shannon burst into my room and plopped onto the bed beside me. As I hastily banged the book shut and turned it over to hide the title, her freakishly puckered lips spoke close to my ear.

"Wut culr luks the west?" Her top lip was blood red and the bottom, fairy pink.

She waited while I had a good laugh. "Well, the pink one matches your fuzzy slippers perfectly," I offered.

Her lips snapped back into their normal shape. "Come on."

"She's healed. It's a miracle."

"You know what I mean." She wore a glittery top the same color as her blue-grey eyes.

"The pink," I said. "Where are you going dressed in that amazing outfit?"

"Rob is taking me to a movie. Do you really think I look amazing?"

I frowned. "Yes, but wasted on Rob."

"I suppose things are moving fast, but..."

I willed myself to calm down so my voice would not betray the shaking inside. "Shannon. He isn't your type."

She sat up on the edge of the bed with a dreamy smile and leaned forward like she was sharing a secret with her best friend. "He's exactly my type. He has goals, he's hard working, he's smart and takes charge. He's so..." She paused, trying to think of the right word.

"Primal?"

She raised her brows. "Yes, primal. How did you think of it?"

"You may be the science genius but that doesn't mean I'm a dummy."

"Nobody ever said that about you."

"Nobody ever says I'm smart, either," I said. "Everybody is always so busy being dazzled by your brilliant mind, I'm pretty much overlooked."

"Overlooked? Ha!" She made her voice low to imitate a male: "Your sister is HOT. Do you think she'll go out with me?"

"When did that happen?" I said.

She tilted her chin. "It's happened."

"Well, you're hot, but you never showed it until now."

"Thanks, but it doesn't count if one's sister thinks you're hot. That's why I like Rob, because he is exciting and wild, and wants me."

Even though I risked more resistance, I didn't want her to keep making a fool of herself. Like the ancient Greek scientist who had to convince his friends the earth is round, not flat, I had to find the courage to tell her the truth.

So I took a deep breath and spilled it all – the buried piece of fur, my conversations with Aunt Althea, my suspicion that the sheep was abducted by a hungry otherworldly creature. I concluded with, "I'm sorry to be the one to tell you this, but it is plausible that Rob is a werewolf."

Her mouth dropped open and closed again. I reassured her, "I don't think he's the devil's spawn. He's just one of the lesser creatures, the kind that made himself into a werewolf."

She searched my face, concern all over hers. "You seem to be serious."

"We don't have a lot of time to debate this, Shannon. Rob is looking for a mate and you are his choice."

She seemed to be considering it, then a look of understanding. "You ARE jealous. You're so used to getting all the male attention you can't stand knowing someone not only likes me better, but you don't even register on his radar. This weird fantasy you've cooked up is crazy, unbelievable, and total character assassination. What exactly do you hope to accomplish?"

"Your safety," I replied as calmly as I could. This was going even worse than I expected.

She reached under the pillow where I had stashed the book. *Secrets of the Wolfen*, she read aloud.

Thumbing through the pages she paused to read the chapter titles: "Origin of the Man Beast...Girls Who Cried Werewolf Too Late... The Mark of the Werewolf..." She closed the book and tossed it back on the bed.

"Time to put away your over-active imagination and join the real world. You're going into your last year in high school! You need to grow up."

She'd been telling me to grow up since I was born so this did not bother me. I instead stuck to the issue.

"I'm going to have to tell Mom and Dad your boyfriend is evil, Shannon."

She expelled one big laugh. "Really? You don't mind ruining their holiday just because you're jealous?"

"Please, listen to reason. Credible sightings of werewolves all over the world have been recorded. They exist. And Rob is acting like one."

She put her hand on my forehead. "Hmm. No fever. So I can only conclude you're either stupid or crazy. Which is it?"

"Probably stupid. For trying to save you. When you think Rob is leaning in to kiss you and he bites you instead and after two days your knuckles start to grow hair – don't come crying to me. Because believe me, I won't be jealous. Werewolf sister."

She raised her finger to her temple and did a slow circle. Then she exited the room with her little freckled nose in the air.

Chapter 16

I was spying at my bedroom window when Rob's SUV pulled up in front and he laid on his horn before sliding out to run up the steps to our door. Shannon emerged a second after he rang the bell.

He chose to impress her by wearing the same jeans and t-shirt style he always wore. Not a man to try to change what worked for him, obviously.

He didn't open her car door for her, but to be fair, I've never seen anybody but Tony with such old fashioned manners. On the other hand, if Rob was as "different" and "mature" as Shannon raved, then he should be more attentive, in my humble opinion. Shannon didn't care though - I saw her face as she slid into the vehicle, a dreamy smile bathed in the beam from our front door light.

For the remainder of the evening I stayed in with Jake. Earlier I had taken him for a little run with me on my bicycle but the summer heat shortened the excursion and at home he relaxed in the cool of my bedroom to gnaw on a new toy. When I took it from him to test for territorial aggression he playfully engaged me in a game of tug. I decided a training session was in order and he followed me downstairs where I retrieved my bag of treats from the kitchen. He learned "drop it" within minutes, and once again I was amazed at how smart and eager to please he was.

I reflected on all his special qualities: He stayed inside the back yard without trying to jump the fence, he never failed to greet me as though we'd been apart for a lifetime, he stayed close when we walked to and from work, he tried to be friends with Shannon even though she didn't like him, and last but not least, he was able to discern the dark beast in Rob.

I told him what an amazing dog he was and he wagged his tail. As training progressed we moved from "drop it" to "fetch" and he caught on to that as well.

I couldn't wait to demonstrate his genius to Shannon. It was getting late so I picked up his rubber chicken and threw it in the toy box by the front door in the living room. As I gathered up another toy, he passed me carrying his tennis ball, which he dropped in the box.

Whether someone taught him this or he imitated me, I couldn't tell, but I was impressed. When I pointed at his stuffed frog on the floor by the sofa, he put it away as well.

"You know, I'm almost convinced you can read my mind."

He licked my hand and I patted him. "If only you could tell me what you know about Rob."

He followed me to my bedroom where I read more of the wolfen book, however, as time stretched out I found it difficult to concentrate. I worried about Shannon going back to Rob's den with him.

By midnight I had finished re-reading the chapter on *Potions for Protection*. Apparently the ancient methods for detection, repelling and eradicating werewolves had remained the same throughout the centuries. Instructions for using monkshood along with an incantation made me realize thousands of animals must have been poisoned during the ongoing battle against shape shifters.

The chapter ended with a crude drawing of a monk holding a huge Bible high in the air in one hand and a crucifix in the other as he faced a man-sized wolfish creature. No explanation accompanied the drawing.

By 1 a.m. Shannon had not returned and I gave up trying to concentrate on anything else. I resisted the urge to phone Tony about my anxiety, knowing the discussion would end in an argument.

An hour later I was close to tears until I heard tires crunching on the gravel outside. Jake gave a little bark and I went to the window.

Relief washed over me. There were two people in the front of Rob's vehicle although thirty-eight and a half minutes crawled by before the passenger door opened and Shannon hopped out. She looked the same as when she left. Human.

When the front door opened I scurried under my bed covers and listened to her heels clump up the stairs and down the hall until they stopped outside my door. She threw it open and flipped on the lights.

"Raine, I saw you in the window."

I sat up. "Why are you so late?"

"Why did you put those purple flowers in my purse?"

"Oh, is he not over his allergy symptoms?"

"He's fine, actually. And I came in here to tell you that you don't have to worry anymore. Rob is the most considerate, sensitive, wonderful guy in the world. He didn't even kiss me. He gave me a sweet hug."

"But did he try to bite you?"

She ignored the question and went to the window to admire the night sky. "Look at all the stars – the weather is so perfect. I think we should throw a big summer party and invite all our friends."

For a moment I got excited because I love parties, but then I remembered that Shannon's idea of a wild party was to stay up late and watch science fiction movies.

"What kind of party?"

"A bonfire. We'll have it at the edge of the orchard at the fire pit."

"Why now after all these years of turning your nose up at my get-togethers with my friends are you Miss Party?"

"Come on – our parents are away for the summer. We're supposed to have a party."

"I didn't see anything about that in the Home Alone Manual."

"Rob suggested we have it in a week and a half on Thursday, the 26th."

I laughed. "Why not a Saturday?"

"Because Thursday is the day of the full moon. The Party Moon."

How quickly amusement can turn to panic. "No! Werewolves change out of their human forms and go on a big tear during full moons."

She grinned. "Exactly."

"No, no, no. Rob would be most dangerous then."

"Listen, I know he seems abrupt, but try to be more understanding. His father abandoned his mom and him when he was only five and his mom left him when he was 16 – he just came home from school one day and she was gone, leaving him to fend for himself. I think he's done an admirable job of carving out a life for himself with virtually no support or encouragement from anyone. He says he's never met a woman as understanding as I am."

I listened to this little heart tugging speech with growing panic. "He has no ties to any human?"

"He's not letting anything hold him back, which is what I like about him. He doesn't feel sorry for himself at all. In fact, he's now focusing on even bigger plans to make a name for himself."

"I can imagine: Local Guy Voted Werewolf Pack Leader."

She took a breath and made an effort to smile. "You're going to have to get used to him whether you like it or not. If everything goes as planned, the night of the bonfire could be big for me." She let that hang in the air with a coy smile playing on her lips and it didn't take a genius to figure out what she meant.

"So. You are planning to throw away something very special for him?"

"What's the big deal?"

"Shannon, please reconsider. You will regret this for the rest of your life."

Her eyes narrowed and an angry edge crept into her voice. "This is my choice, Raine. Save your sanctimony." She turned and left.

I wiped my eyes with my bed quilt and tried to clear my thoughts. Rob's werewolf charm was strong and Shannon seemed unable to resist it. I needed to consult with Aunt Althea again.

Chapter 17

"He is practiced at being human, this Rob." Aunt Althea studied the sweet snack in her hand as if it held the key to Rob's true identity. "Maybe he doesn't know he is a werewolf – perhaps the transformation seems like a dream to him." She bit into the treat and munched slowly.

We were sitting by the pool in the shade of the umbrella. Tony was off checking the support ties on the trees in our orchard. He didn't know I was here because I didn't want to talk about my suspicions with him anymore than I had to.

I had walked over with Jake who stayed near me until we got close to the Callas' house, then he bounded off toward the north pasture which was hidden by the crest of a hill. Since Sassy hadn't run to greet us I knew Jake must be looking for her and I let him go. I was comfortable with my dog's loyalty and knew he would come back if I called.

When I arrived at the house Althea seemed pleased to see me and seized the opportunity to bring out a heaping platter of fresh baking. Since I had just eaten lunch, I did not have any, but she didn't care and ate two cookies. She savored both the mystery of Rob's identity and the sweet goods.

She eyed me shrewdly. "There is something more?"

I described Shannon's attraction to him but left out the part about my sister planning to give herself to him.

"Shannon changed so fast," I said and could not keep the sadness from my voice.

She watched as I attempted to swallow my worry with iced tea. "You don't know your sister as well as you thought you did."

She was right, but that didn't help the current situation. "I've been reading the book you gave me. It describes a ritual for exorcising the werewolf spirit. The trick is to lure him inside a special circle. I propose to lure him into the circle then you perform the exorcism."

She looked aghast. "He could attack both of us long before he got inside a circle."

"I was hoping you would know how to overcome that problem."

She finished off her snack and brushed her hands together. "I do. Wait here."

She went back into the house and quickly returned with two little vials in her hand, one of them wrapped in a piece of paper. She ordered me to stand up and while mumbling in Greek, waved one of the vials at me. Drops of something pleasant-smelling landed on my head and trickled down my scalp. The ritual took about one minute, after which she returned to her chair and put the two vials on the table.

I wiped the trickles from my forehead and inhaled the scent on the back of my hand. "What is this?"

"Lavender. It will charm the wolf and keep him from tearing you to pieces. The other is colloidal silver."

"Why couldn't I have put lavender under my pillow earlier instead of the foul herb bag?"

"The herb bag was to stop a werewolf from entering your room to claim you as a mate. Since it has become clear he wants Shannon, YOU must protect yourself from being harmed if you get in the way."

"What a relief."

She waved her hand dismissively. "The beast must swallow the liquid silver so he will cough up the wolf demon and turn back into his human form."

"Like a silver bullet?"

"No. The silver bullet is a Hollywood myth."

"Too bad. Getting him to swallow some strange concoction doesn't sound much easier than luring him into a circle."

"The lavender charm will slow him down. Put the silver in something he likes to drink and offer it to him. The incantation is on the paper." She stopped me when I reached for the vial. "Do not recite the words until right before the procedure or some of the power will be lost."

Clutching the vial in my hand a part of me was acutely aware that I was putting a lot of trust in an old woman who could be crazy. Another part of me thought I had no choice, and a deeper part of me wondered if there was better protection than rituals and potions linked to superstitions from the dark ages.

"When should I do this?"

"As soon as possible."

"Before the full moon?"

"Yes."

I shuddered.

She pushed the plate of baking toward me and urged me to try it with a wink. "It has magic to calm you."

"That would be great."

By the glint in her eye I wondered if she meant romance and that made me think of Tony. Then, as if called up by my thoughts, I heard him talking to someone. The gate swung open and he strode in followed by Sassy and Jake.

Althea took the empty pitcher into the house for more tea.

The dogs ran ahead of him to the naked boy fountain and took turns lapping up water. Tony settled under the umbrella beside me with a grin.

"Hey," I said, awkwardly.

"What are you doing here?"

"It's a hot day. I was hoping for an invite for a swim."

"You don't have to wait for an invitation."

I smiled, a wave of shyness erasing my ability to speak intelligently. Instead I stripped off my shorts and top to the one-piece suit underneath, and reveled in Tony's shy appreciation. He didn't take long to run into the house, change into shorts, and run back out. We both enjoyed a swim and there was no more talk of potions and werewolves that afternoon.

Chapter 18

"We can't both fit on that seat."

"You want seating to be snug on these things for safety." Tony's expression was too innocent to be genuine.

His cherry red motorcycle shimmered under the afternoon sun, all sparkle chrome and leather. I knew he rode all over the valley on it, but when he buzzed into our driveway to take me to the dog obedience rally I was annoyed.

He had invited me the day before and I looked forward to our first official date, sitting next to him while he leaned close to explain the dogs' performances. I didn't tell him Shannon and Rob were also attending.

"My mother would not approve of this. Where's your truck?" I said, eyeing the bike.

He grinned. "Let's not tell her."

"I'm not afraid," I insisted. "Just concerned about the lack of...room."

He gave me a knowing smile and handed me a helmet that matched his, shimmer red with black racing stripes. The expression in his eyes was too hot to handle and I turned my head slightly to hitch the strap under my chin.

"Do you want to put that in here?" he said eyeing my fanny pack and opening the cubby below the seat.

The bag sticking out from my stomach lowered my cool factor a lot, but it was handier than a purse on a motorcycle and I needed a place for my cell phone, mini binoculars and water. I dropped it in the cubby. He settled on the seat and kicked the machine into an ear-splitting roar. He ordered me to get on and I slid in behind him, so thankful he couldn't see my flaming cheeks.

"Feet up here," he yelled over the din and motioned to the tiny foot rests behind his, one on each side. "If you think you're going to fall, put your arms around me."

I sat as straight as I could, holding onto seat bars on the side.

"All set?"

A second later the motorbike raced down our driveway at what seemed like a crazy speed. We turned onto the main road and into regular traffic. I felt small and vulnerable. At the same time a rush of exhilaration flowed through my body and I let out a scream of delight. In the joy of the moment I hugged his waist unabashedly. In spite of the noise of the wind and helmet covering my ears, I heard him laugh.

We arrived about 20 minutes later at the arena. Under the artificial lighting in the cavernous building all the spectators were the same color as the buttered popcorn but I soon spotted Shannon and Rob. They huddled together on the second bench up from the front, Shannon's orange-topped head turned toward Rob while he watched a Shetland Sheepdog owning the obedience course. Her face radiated happiness. I had never seen her so animated.

I wanted to be glad for her but the reason for her transformation prevented me. I couldn't see Rob's face when he leaned in to speak into her ear, but the intimate gesture jacked up the urgency of my mission.

We were close enough for her to view us, should she happen to tear her puppy eyes off of Rob, so I clutched at Tony's hand and tried to lead the way up to the shadowed back bleachers.

He wrapped his hand around mine willingly, but stood his ground. "Let's sit in the space right over there behind that couple. Hey, it's your sister and Rob." He turned to me.

"Okay, I knew they would be here."

"Why didn't you tell me?"

"I didn't know until after you invited me," I fibbed. "But yeah, I don't want them to know I'm here."

I let go of his hand and took the steps up to the back bleachers two at a time. He followed and plunked down beside me.

"So you can spy on them?"

I faced forward and pretended to be mesmerized by the competition. After a moment he apologized. "I don't want to mess up our date."

"Neither do I."

"Do you want to go?"

"No. I really to want to watch the dogs."

"Okay."

A kid selling snacks ventured up our way and Tony bought two bottles of soda and a giant box of popcorn. We had shared snacks between us many times over the years yet this time it felt like something more. The dog competition, as well as Shannon and Rob faded into the background of my awareness.

"Is it hot in here?" I said.

"A little."

After a while he asked, "Do you think he's going to start snarling and foaming in front of all these people?"

It took me a moment to understand what he was talking about. Although we were pretty much by ourselves in the high section of the arena, I leaned closer to him and spoke quietly. "Shannon is planning...er...Shannon is not herself."

His dark eyes studied mine. "She's 19. It's not up to you to police her."

My face burned and I turned back to the action in the arena.

Another dog and master pair entered the ring. The loud speaker crackled to life and announced their names.

"What do you think of the dogs?" he asked. "Impressive, aren't they?"

I agreed with him and for a moment forgot our quarrel. "Jake is a genius dog. He could do this."

Tony chuckled. "He's too big. He would terrify the sheep."

Before the dog in the ring had completed his course, Rob and Shannon got up. My instincts took over and I grabbed Tony's hand. "They're leaving. We've got to follow them."

He pulled out of my grasp and stayed sitting. "No."

"Please, Tony. We can stay back out of sight. They won't be any the wiser and..." I had to think fast. "...and I love riding on your bike."

Chapter 19

Rob obeyed the speed limit so we had no trouble keeping up to his SUV with a couple of cars between us as they crossed the Lake Bridge and straight to the industrial area north of the city. We would have been easy to spot if Shannon had once taken her eyes off Rob and turned around to look.

The SUV turned into the alley beside the Alpha Guy Dog Training Center and drove two and a half blocks until it came to another street, crossed, and pulled in front of a large storage building seperated by a chain link fence surrounding two smaller sheds. A small cheap sign above the center door, painted a bright yellow, identified it as Alpha Den Dog Boarding.

Tony eased up behind a dumpster and stopped with the engine idling. I concentrated on my goal to keep Shannon in sight. She and Rob left the vehicle and went into the boarding kennel. Rob walked in ahead of her so she had to catch the door.

The dogs inside barked at them, a noise that echoed across the valley.

"Okay, now you know where they are. Can we go for an ice cream or do you want to go home?"

I dismounted and pulled off my helmet. "I have to know what he's up to. What if Shannon needs help?"

He tapped his leather-gloved fingers on the bike handle.

"Tony, even if you don't believe in werewolves, I believe human Rob was sneaking around in our orchard the other day and he has a weird, unhealthy power over Shannon. I can't relax until I figure out what he is up to with my sister."

"But you didn't bring Aunt Althea's werewolf repellent bags. How are you going to save Shannon?"

I pretended I didn't recognize his sarcasm. "Don't worry, I brought something." Aunt Althea's vial of liquid silver was inside a pink change purse in the fanny pack.

He lost his smirk. "What did you bring?"

"I don't have to tell you."

"Get back on or I will leave without you."

I won't lie, his disapproval was hard to take. Even if he was bluffing, giving me an ultimatum was kind of harsh. We had always been friends and to explore a new kind of relationship was something I wanted. I looked into his eyes trying to gauge if he would really leave me stranded and after a moment the scowl disappeared, and he unfolded his arms.

"How can you expect me to give up on my sister when I think she might be in danger?" I pleaded.

He took my hand. "Rainy, she's not in danger. I asked Nick about him and he said Rob is eccentric but he is great with dogs. Why would he risk his reputation in this town by harming your sister? Why don't you try to accept that he is attracted to her? It's really not that hard to believe."

Tony seemed to be softening a little. So I resisted the urge to remind him that I believed Rob had a dark uncontrollable element to his character that would override cop-approved Rob for sure.

I looked to the door Shannon had followed Rob into and wrestled with indecision. I supposed that I could come back later.

Tony's lips offered a faint encouraging smile. Did I really want to be skulking around here when I could be with someone I really wanted to be with? I think of myself as eccentric, but not crazy.

Tony visibly relaxed when I smiled and put my helmet on. But just as I was about to swing my leg behind him, a loud mournful howl shook the air around us, rising in intensity then settling into a sad wail until dying by degrees. It came from one of the two sheds although I could not pinpoint which one. Then the chorus of kenneled dogs from within the main building replied.

I removed my helmet again and scrutinized the property for movement. "That sounded a lot like the howl I heard in our orchard."

"A wolf for sure," he said in a hushed voice.

We waited for a few minutes more.

"Tony, I have to see that wolf."

"No. It could be dangerous."

"Exactly. Up until now I thought I could be wrong about Aunt Althea's wolfen and that Rob is just an unpleasant guy with some quirks. But now...I'm really sure he could be dangerous, no matter what else is going on. He's got a wolf and they were in our orchard two weeks ago. Now he's got Shannon. I can't leave. Whether she appreciates it or not, I've got to save her from...whatever is going on here."

"I'll take a bus home – no hard feelings." I stepped away from him and turned toward the building that Rob and Shannon had entered. I kept walking without looking back. After a moment I felt Tony beside me.

"If we get out of this without being busted for stalking, I'm going to have a talk with Aunt Althea about putting ideas into your head. 15 minutes. I mean it."

"15 minutes - unless I have to do a werewolf intervention," I said and scurried to the closest window and flattened myself next to it. Carefully I rose to peek in, ready to drop if anyone looked my way.

Inside a tall young woman, with a long blond French braid, and jeans tucked into rubber boots, worked a German Shepherd in the center area. Dogs of all sizes peered out of large kennels surrounding them. One or two barked, a couple whined, but the woman ignored the noise while she put the shepherd through a series of commands.

Both the trainer and dog were impressive and for a moment I forgot my mission until Tony nudged me. I stepped aside so he could look.

He swore. "Where is your sister? She's going to find us, Raine."

I pondered our position. Rob and Shannon must have exited the building through the back door, but where did they go?

Then another howl rose up, coming the closest shed about 50 feet away. Expecting Tony to follow, I headed for a gap in the fencing between it and the main building. I sprinted over to the shed and flattened against the outside wall beside a large dirty pane. Slowly I eased around to look in.

I stifled a gasp. Rob and Shannon were there, but they were not alone. An enormous black wolf paced inside a large cage while Rob stood admiring him. The beast must have been at least 200 pounds, and I could see Shannon was as alarmed as I was, however, when Rob turned to her she smiled.

At the same time, the animal sensed my presence and it's cold yellow eyes looked straight into mine. I dropped to the ground below the window and the wolf growled. Rob spoke to it in a soothing voice.

The werewolf's lair? I took the vial of silver out of my pack and concealed it in my hand. I looked around for Tony but he wasn't anywhere near me. Instead he was still on the other side of the fence, not quite able to squeeze through the gap I had come through although he was still squirming.

What could I do? Tell him to suck in his six pack? "Go around," I hissed. But he continued to struggle. "Really, I'll be okay. Go look for another opening."

He stopped moving, face as red as Shannon's new hair color. "Uh, Raine?" he paused, out of breath. "I'm stuck."

I scooted back toward him and in my haste tripped over a partially buried bone and plowed into him. The collision was enough to push him back on the other side of the fence but at that moment, the back door of the larger building squawked open, and the woman and her shepherd emerged. We were in her line of vision if she turned our way. "Move!" Tony said as he sprinted away. I slid around the side of the building and crouched behind a big waste bin. The bin obscured my position from her, but if Rob and Shannon came out they would trip over me.

The lid of the bin was open, leaving a crack between the hinges and a small view of the woman and dog as they trotted the short distance toward the main building. I held my breath. Tony had disappeared. I could do nothing but wait for her to go inside, not moving even when flies buzzed around my face. Suddenly the dog sensed something and looked my way.

What a stupid situation. If I got caught like this and word got around everyone would think I was a loser for spying on my sister and I would never be able to hold my head up again – unless it turned out Rob was a werewolf. I couldn't decide which was worse.

Where was Tony? Did he escape? "Please please please...don't let him get in trouble because of me," I prayed.

Then the dog switched its focus and started barking and pulling at its leash and after a moment I could see Tony as he strolled toward the woman.

"Hey there," he called out with a friendly smile. She quieted her dog.

I wasted no time making my escape. I scurried around the other side of the shed, and then bolted for the back of the building. Once out of sight, I scrambled over the fence, a feat that would have been harder had I not had so much adrenalin pumping through my muscles. I moved to the other side of the fence with the shed between me and the woman's line of vision. Near the street I slowed to speed walk – at that point she wouldn't know I had been inside the property – and made my way to Tony's motorbike in the alley. I hunched behind the Ming Restaurant dumpster, inhaling the odor of old grease and exhaling another prayer that Shannon and Rob would not leave the shack until Tony was gone.

After a long five minutes of chatting, Tony and the woman parted. She and the dog continued their jog down the street and Tony sprinted away in the opposite direction. I watched until he turned at the end of the block and disappeared. About 10 minutes later he crept up behind me.

"Let's go."

I jumped and hit my head on the lip of the dumpster.

"Come on," he said. "Your 15 minutes expired a long time ago."

Rubbing the bump, I tried to figure out what to do. I did not want to abandon Shannon in the wolf's den.

Before I could decide, Shannon and Rob exited the shed and headed for the back of the other kennel building where we had been. She was babbling on like a girl with a crush – thank heavens. She glanced once in our direction, but I didn't think she saw us. She was so focused on Rob who, with his loping walk and wild hair looked as though he might shape shift at any moment. When she stopped to adjust her sandal, right in front of the fence gap where Tony had been stuck, he chided her for wearing "inappropriate" shoes and to my disgust she agreed and apologized. *She's already under his spell.* Then they disappeared behind the building, re-emerged through the front door and got into his vehicle. I let out a lung full of air I hadn't realized I was holding. Since he wouldn't be able to drive with wolfen paws, I figured she was still safe for a while.

Once they were out of sight, Tony put on his helmet and handed me mine. "I hope you've had enough."

"Who was that woman?"

He looked pained. "She's on Nick's softball team. Her name is Kayla and apparently she works for Rob part-time."

"How did you explain being here?"

"I asked about dog boarding fees."

"What are they?"

"Let's just go."

"Tony, Rob has a big black wolf locked up in that shed."

"So? A few people keep them as pets. We discussed that."

"But..."

"We'll talk about it later."

"Okay, but I'm not giving up on exposing the truth that I know in my heart. And saving my sister."

"Ok." He ended the discussion with the roar of the motor bike.

Chapter 20

Instead of taking me straight home, Tony detoured to a highway petting zoo/ice cream shop. When we arrived a big tour bus parked in front was disgorging about a hundred chattering Japanese tourists who already formed a growing line inside the shop. I did not mind his decision to stop there because I wanted him to be sweetened up before I brought up the wolf again. Besides, I like ice cream.

I studied the list of 150 flavors on the white boards high on the wall behind the employees' heads, aware of Tony's less than cheerful disposition.

"You may disagree with what I did, but I'm trying to save my sister from making a big mistake," I said.

I sensed him give in a little. "She won't listen to you if you keep acting this way. She likes Rob. You need inarguable proof that he is dangerous."

"Like what?"

"I don't know. Photos of him changing into a beast?" He chuckled. I couldn't be sure if he was starting to believe or not.

Once we were settled at a picnic table outside with our three-decker cones I asked, "Why do you think he keeps a wolf?"

He licked up a large chunk of his top scoop before answering. "I'm no psychotherapist but I'm pretty sure he's like lots of guys. It makes him feel more macho. More powerful. It's the same as any guy with a dangerous dog. But it doesn't matter what I think, does it? Why do YOU think he has one?"

He took another big messy slurp and I decided his cone eating technique was not one of his most attractive features. Yet a girl at the next table looked his way with interest in spite of his stupid ice cream mustache. I frowned at her.

He grinned a goofy grin. "You think he shares a body with a wolf. Right?"

"Don't try smirking with ice cream on your face," I said.

"Rob's pet wolf could be the one who stole your sheep. That should concern you."

He grabbed a napkin and wiped away his mustache. Okay, he did look kind of adorable, however, I did not like his attitude.

His cone was already half gone while mine had begun to melt. I licked the rivulets off my hand.

"Maybe, but why didn't Sassy bark?"

"That beast is huge, Tony. She choked with fear."

"I don't know. But doesn't this weaken your werewolf theory rather than support it?"

Instead of pointing out that the wolf and Rob could be the same, I tried the middle road. "I'm willing to consider every possible explanation for a lot of weird occurrences."

As he finished his cone, I unzipped my pack for a tissue. Then I remembered the little pink vial with Aunt Althea's potion. It wasn't in the fanny pack. Panicked, I felt my pocket. Gone.

"What's wrong?"

"Nothing." I had lost interest in ice cream.

"Are you planning to finish that before it melts all over you?"

I handed it to him and he devoured it in a few bites. "Why don't you just ask Rob about the wolf?"

"I'll talk to Shannon. My next plan will be based on her response." I thought back to my movements when I was at Rob's. But in all the dashing and running around, I couldn't be sure where I dropped it. If Rob found it, would he be able to connect it to me?

Thinking about my escape I had to acknowledge that without Tony's help I would have been in big trouble, but when I thanked him he wasn't pleased.

"You're going to leave me out of any more of your spy plans, right?"

That he considered my actions to be spying rather than protection bothered me. "Don't worry, I can handle the rest alone." But I was not so confident since I wondered if the werewolf's supernatural power caused me to lose the vial.

He lifted a skeptical brow. "The rest of what?"

"I..."

"Never mind. I don't even want to know."

Chapter 21

The pleasant aroma of sizzling bacon enveloped me as soon as I got home, and for a moment I forgot our mother was away. In the kitchen two place settings, syrup and butter, and a platter of bacon beckoned. Shannon stood at the counter stirring pancake batter, her damp hair from a recent shower, pajama pants and a thin-strapped teddy giving her an aura of delicate femininity that I had never noticed in her before. When she heard me approach she spoke cheerily over her shoulder. "Hungry? Supper is about ready."

Since I hadn't eaten much ice cream, my stomach still had room for my favorite meal, and Shannon's domestic puttering was too homey to resist.

"What's the occasion?" I asked.

"We have to talk."

Had she come to her senses about Rob? Hope energized me as I anticipated the pancakes and our sisters bonding time - until she poured batter onto the griddle and flashed a black fur wrist band. It dangled on her wrist and slid with her movements. Taunting me.

I tried to speak through the panic constricting my throat. "Rob gave you his watch," I said.

She smiled with dreamy eyes. "Yes. It's not pretty but so symbolic of everything Rob, don't you think?"

"What do you mean?"

"A streak of wild energy seething just below the surface. The black symbolizes his inner power."

She was getting closer to the real Rob. "It doesn't go with anything you wear." I retrieved the milk from the fridge and filled our glasses as I tried to think of a way to tell her the bracelet turned innocent maidens into angry she-wolves.

She flipped a pancake. "It's part of Rob, so it goes with everything. He told me I must never take it off. Put out the knives and forks, would you?"

My mind churned trying to remember the ancient words in *Secrets of the Wolfen,* the shape shifters chant. "Uh, did he give you a...a poem to go with it?"

"No, he's not mushy."

"Did he mumble something you couldn't quite understand when he gave it to you?"

She ignored me and hummed a love tune.

I was so distracted by the impending crisis that I opened the cutlery drawer and put my hand in to grab forks without looking. Instead of the cool feel of stainless steel, my fingers alighted on a small round cylinder. I pulled back, knowing with a sinking of my stomach what it was.

Shannon plopped a pancake on each of our plates. "Did something bite you?" she asked innocently. My mind flashed back to her stopping in front of the place where I had tripped. She must have seen it on the ground and slipped it into her pocket.

I picked out the vial, bare without it's little scrap of paper. I lifted my chin.

"Where did you get this?"

Her eyes narrowed. "I saw you there, dear sister. Spying on us. When I saw this weird thing it wasn't hard to put 2 and 2 together."

"You always were the math whiz."

She dropped the skillet in the sink with a clang, the sound echoing throughout the kitchen, and reached into the pocket of her pajama pants to bring out the paper. After making some sort of profound point by scowling at me for a moment, she read out loud:

"Foul canine release this person's soul, return to the great black hole."

I cringed. What uncontrolled power had she now released and where would it land? She started to read again but I sprung at her and clapped my hand over her mouth. "Shannon, stop it. You don't know what you're doing."

She pulled my hand away and tore the paper into little bits, letting them float to the floor. Without another word she sat at the table and poured syrup on her pancake, picked up her fork, and ripped four jagged claw-like lines across the soggy cake in an alarmingly violent manner. Had the incantation awakened a foul canine in her?

"I can't believe you were spying on me. What were you thinking? What did you expect to accomplish besides humiliating me in front of Rob? And the worst of it is, you managed to talk that love sick Tony into helping you."

"He's not love sick."

She gave a short, mirthless laugh. "Is defending Tony's state of mind the most important thing to you right now? I demand an explanation. And I know this is going to be good." She rested her elbows on the table and waited.

I couldn't tear my eyes from that ugly piece of fur. "Shannon, I know this seems like illogical behavior..."

She snorted. "Try insane."

"I'm trying to watch you, in case you need help."

"Your concern is baseless."

"Why does Rob keep a wolf at his kennel? Those animals should not be domesticated."

"Not that it's any of your business, but he studies all canines to help him develop his training techniques. He's had that wolf since it was a cub. He told me they are like brothers."

"Yes. They would be. Is the watchband fur from his pet?"

"As a matter of fact, hairs from the tail were woven together. Why are you obsessing over it?"

She stroked the fur with her thumb, waiting for an answer. I wanted to tell her to stop, because stroking could stir up who knows what kind of evil forces from hell, but she already considered me unsound. Since she remained stubbornly unmoved by the actual evidence, she wouldn't believe me when I told her that in ancient times wolf's fur donned during a full moon and accompanied by an oath to the devil changed a man into a werewolf.

For sure she would scoff if I tried to explain that Rob had given her the bracelet to seal her as his wolf woman.

Even in my own head it played like a bad horror movie. I chewed on a pancake that didn't need chewing, and tried to say something reasonable. "Mmm. These are the best pancakes ever. Better than Mom's even."

I could see the wheels turning in her head as she ate. She swallowed. "Raine, thank you for caring enough to worry about me but I want you to stop doing weird stuff. I got a text message from Mom saying they would be phoning at 6, in one hour. If you don't promise to drop this werewolf obsession, I'm going to have to ask them to speak to you about it."

First she seemed to wise up and understand I only had her best interests at heart, and then she turned back into the clueless girlfriend of Alpha Guy.

"If you tell them anything bad about me, I'll tell them about the big bonfire party you plan to have."

She waved her fork at me. "Promise to stop spying on me and Rob."

"Okay, if Jake and I can quit obedience lessons." I was pretty sure she would go for this because she didn't need a pretense to see him now, and hopefully the cost issue was long forgotten in the fog of her infatuation.

"If you pay me back my half. $150."

"I'll give you $200 to give up Rob."

Her eyes widened. "You're serious?"

"Yes." I swallowed. A year of part-time jobs had earned enough for me to save $3500 toward a well-kept little yellow car Mr. Buckner planned to sell for $5500. He had promised to hold it until the end of the summer. I didn't want to rely on Shannon for rides anymore - especially now since Tony had offered to teach me to drive. I took a deep breath. Shannon's well-being – and humanness - was more important than a car.

She easily declined, oblivious to my willingness to make such a sacrifice. "Just give me the $150."

The injustice burned, beginning in my stomach and rising up to my cheeks. "Rob is the one who should pay the money back. Jake and I did not learn one thing from him. In fact, the only useful instruction Rob came up with was to give Jake more exercise, while his actual contact has only agitated the dog. Rob is the only person Jake growls at."

In spite of her protests I stormed out to the back yard and returned with Jake. I had a couple of dried liver treats in my pocket and I stood in front of him and ordered him to "say your prayers". Immediately he dropped to his belly with head on the floor and crossed his paws.

"Yes!" I tossed him a treat and he caught it in the air.

"Can't you agree? He is easy to train using positive reinforcement rather than punishment and abuse."

Her expression revealed the conflict she felt. She didn't like to admit when I was right, which didn't happen often anyway according to her.

"Okay, but will he sit without a treat or are you going to have to keep pieces of food in your pocket for the rest of his life?"

"Hey, he's a work in progress. At least he hasn't been jumping all over you or even the furniture lately. Haven't you noticed?"

She started to say something more but I interrupted her. "Wait. Look at this."

Jake was still sitting, eagerly waiting for more of this fun game. I looked down at him with the biggest fake smile I could produce and through my teeth said, "Smile. Smile, Jake."

He worked at pulling his lips back from his teeth and finally produced the cutest doggy snarl/smile ever. I encouraged him to "keep smiling and wave at Shannon". He raised a paw and waved.

"Yes! Isn't he amazing?" He caught my last treat as it arced in the air.

"How did you get him to do that?" she asked.

"Jake is easy to train in spite of what Rob says."

Shannon held up her hand. "Okay, okay. I don't see the point in putting us all through continuing conflict." She couldn't resist flashing a fake smile at Jake and laughed at what she got in return. I didn't have anymore liver so I stole a piece of bacon from her plate and gave it to him.

She didn't look at me as she pushed her plate away with only two bites out of the pancake. Her makeover must have included a diet. I reached out to snatch the remaining bacon but she caught my wrist and held my eyes.

"No more spying, okay?"

I pulled out of her grasp. "Ok."

I was not lying when I agreed not to spy, because I had never spied. I was *guarding* her. I counted on Aunt Althea for more silver and another incantation.

Chapter 22

"Wow, I hardly recognize my little Shanny."

"Good. So please call me Shannon instead?"

Dad looked surprised. She had never snapped at him about his pet name for her before.

"Is anything wrong, Honey?" Even on our tablet we could see Mom's expression etched with that common brand of inquisitiveness disguised as motherly concern.

Shannon realized her mistake and changed the subject. "Mom, you would not believe how well things are going here. Raine and I haven't quarreled over chores once, the program committee at the recreation center loves my science camp, and I purchased a new wardrobe for university."

In Athens the time was past 2 am, yet both our parents appeared rejuvenated. They accepted Shannon's report without comment and told us all about their explorations and discoveries in the amazing country of Greece. Normally I would have been hanging on every description but right now there was a big distraction I couldn't shake.

"Any other news? Raine? Your hair looks the same," Dad said.

I avoided a glance at Shannon. "It's still working for me."

My Dad is a great guy. When we were little he bought each of us a little go-cart and packed down paths through our orchard for us to tear around on. He loved watching us as much as we enjoyed playing. He was our loudest (and sometime most embarrassing) cheerleader at our sports competitions and he always encouraged us no matter what we wanted to do. He was as proud of my soccer wins as he was of Shannon's science fair projects.

However, we usually took our problems to Mom, who's favorite word is "resourceful". She has always conquered problems both at home and at her wig shop using her resourcefulness. Even though I couldn't tell her about Rob and Shannon, I knew what her advice would be.

Dad asked how the trees looked. Shannon said "fine" and I described the fruit-heavy branches and Tony's work to keep them up. I assured him Tony was unfailingly conscientious, which brought up another topic.

"Tony told his parents you and Althea hit it off, Raine." Dad said.

"I enjoy her stories," I agreed.

This drew a cynical snicker from Shannon.

Dad ignored her. "Honey, don't let any of Althea's stories spook you. She's got a lot of good old country herbal remedies for things like colds and warts, but beyond that her ideas are out there."

Mom nodded in agreement.

Poor Althea. She had to deal with this sort of skepticism too.

"Tony told me the same thing."

"You listen to him. That young man has a good head on his shoulders."

"Big head, you mean."

He laughed. "He's still a fine person. You could do worse than date him."

I didn't know how to answer him but Mom gave me a knowing look and changed the subject. "How is Jake coming along with obedience training?"

Shannon and I started talking at once.

"Rob is an excellent trainer...".

"Jake is doing great."

"Good..." Mom's voice held a question. She knew us well enough to sense something else going on.

"Obedience training is over but Shannon enjoys dating Rob," I said. I sensed my sister tense up, however Mom seemed pleased by the news. Could it be that behind all her bragging about Shannon's brilliance she was a bit worried about her lack of a social life?

Shannon took the opportunity to prepare them. "He is the smartest and most mature guy I have ever met," she gushed. "You both will love him when you meet him. He's got a great business and he's writing a dog training book which I'm sure will be a best seller." She proceeded to describe all his gloriousness. It was clever of her to throw in his business skills since that was guaranteed to impress Mom. Maybe she wouldn't mind his wolfish qualities either.

But after my sister finished talking about Rob, neither parent offered further comment. Instead Dad wound down by asking me to clean up the picker's cabin at the back of our orchard in case we had to hire more help in the fall. He signed off with a cheerful "Be careful, be good, and be happy."

Yes, they were tranquil in Greece.

Afterward, I still had ice cream, pancakes and bacon to work off so I decided to jog up to the cabin. With sunset about an hour away, Jake and I followed the thin trail at the edge of the property and headed north, up the hill. Jake leaped ahead, while I jogged at a steady pace. Soft light and quiet descended upon the valley bathing everything in dusky beauty.

I usually loved this time of day, but now my thoughts were edged with uneasiness and I wondered if any supernatural creature could step out from behind an invisible curtain between the rows of trees. Werewolves were creatures of the night and unlikely to appear in full form at dusk, nevertheless, I stayed alert to all possibilities.

Within 15 minutes we reached the cabin, a small structure in need of paint and fronted by a few hardy perennials. Jake bounded to the door and barked as if ordering an inhabitant to let us in. A scolding magpie materialized out of nowhere and alighted on a dead tree nearby.

Loud bleating greeted me as I pushed open the creaking door. Inside a little lamb skittered away and bleated again. I ordered Jake to stay outside and pulled my cell phone out of my pocket.

Tony arrived about 15 minutes later with a backpack and a baby bottle of water. "She looks okay to me – she's even bigger. I'd say someone has been looking after her." He gently felt the lamb's ribs and nodded relief.

Jake whined outside echoing my unease. The sun was now almost completely behind the western hills – only its dying rays reached up to leave a faint light – and I wanted to get going.

"Who would have a reason to keep a lamb not far from where it was stolen?" I spoke quietly, almost a whisper. The thief might still be around – and not friendly.

He straightened and studied our surroundings. Someone had swept away the inevitable dust and debris which gathers in empty shacks. Two bunk frames, an old chair, a water bucket and a feed bucket furnished the space.

"I've got nothin'," he said.

"Me too." I couldn't think of a motive for Rob, human or otherwise.

Tony retrieved a lantern flashlight from the backpack then strapped the lamb inside and hoisted it to his back. "Let's leave everything alone and get out of here."

Jake was scratching at the trunk of a dead jack pine tree and I called him but he ignored me. Marks in the bark caught my attention.

"Tony..." I said.

He was about to head off down the trail. "What's wrong?"

I motioned for him. The expression on my face quickened his steps. He squinted at the trunk in the dimming light, then unclipped the flashlight from his belt and shone it on three deep parallel gouges in the grey bark.

"What the..." he whispered.

While the lamb bleated and squirmed, and the magpie threw in some screeches for good measure, Tony studied the marks. He put his hand over the lines and compared them, the outside two about six inches long with the inside line slightly longer. Reading my mind – which at this point wasn't too hard – he said, "Wolves don't do this sort of thing."

"Remember when Jake chased your cat up the tree? He jumped up on the trunk. A wolf might do that too."

"Jake didn't leave any marks, did he? And these are too far apart to be from any wolf, no matter how big."

"A MAN wolf could. And Rob has been in this orchard on at least one occasion. You said yourself no one would be able to move around the sheep pen without Sassy raising an alarm. Rob is a dog trainer. Even in his human form he might have the skill."

He considered. "For what purpose?"

"Same reason you used to keep cheese crackers under your bed."

"Huh?"

"You wanted snacks always available."

"You remember that?"

I put a calming hand on the lamb but I couldn't stifle a little shiver of my own. "Let's go before it is completely dark."

He held up the lantern and we followed him down the path.

"At least the sky is clear." He pointed up to the almost-full moon hanging in the grey pink sky like a pendant and I felt the eyes of the werewolf clan watching us from some shadowed place, waiting for total darkness.

"You should keep an open mind at least," I said, needing the sound of my voice to fill the gloom.

"Not for werewolves."

"What about the legends of your people, those old Greek legends? How could the stories survive for hundreds of years if there wasn't some truth to them?"

"Apparently, 'my people' were bored in the evenings. They entertained each other by making up freaks."

"Or they tuned into the supernatural world because they didn't have other distractions."

"I'm going to call Nick. He'll get Fish and Wildlife to come out here and provide a reasonable theory."

I welcomed having professionals investigate and tell my sister and Tony that no natural creature could have made those scratches.

He read my mind. "Bears claw trees."

"Don't they make four marks? Besides, bears don't come around until the fruit is ripe."

"If we're looking at mythical creatures as possible culprits, then we also have to consider Bigfoot."

I scowled at his back. "I wish your funny jokes made us safe."

Dark descended as the lights of our farms came into view from our position on the hill. The trail split and to the right it wound through the orchard to my home but as Tony continued to the left, I followed his light all the way to his farm.

Chapter 23

Tony fussed over the lamb and its mother in the pen for several minutes, relieved that she accepted her baby back. Before we left he re-checked the security of the locks and ordered Sassy to guard her flock.

"Nobody is getting in here tonight," he muttered. He went to his pick-up truck parked not far away and opened the rear gate for Jake to jump in.

I hesitated. "I want to hear what Aunt Althea has to say about this."

The bulb from atop the barn door bathed the yard in thin light. I felt rather than saw his disapproval. "She has a TV show she likes to watch on Saturday nights."

I checked my phone for the time - it was already after nine. A million stars beamed from the navy sky, the kind of night I loved to be out in, but not now – I was too fearful. And I didn't want to be.

I secured Jake's leash. "This won't take long."

I started toward the house, and Tony had no choice but to follow.

Inside he called for her. She came out of her room dressed in black silk pajamas with large pink bunny slippers on her feet, and smelling faintly of earth and pine. She held a book with her finger inside to mark her page. The title on the faded jacket was *Modern Magic and Herbs*.

"Snacks in kitchen," she said.

I knew Tony didn't want to tell her anything, but after a quick glance my way he spilled it. "Raine found the lamb in the picker's cabin at the back of the orchard. Somebody has been feeding it there."

For a moment she stared at him as if she didn't understand what he said.

"We also saw the mark of the wolfen," I added. I clawed the air with three fingers - an air sign of my own. "Right outside the cabin. Did he make the mark to warn people away from the lamb?"

The book slipped from her fingers and she dropped down into the nearest wingback chair. Indecipherable words rolled from her lips.

"Aunty! Are you okay?"

Her eyes fluttered and Tony ran to get her water. "Marks?" she murmured. The color had drained from her face. "It can't be."

Her obvious fright was not reassuring, nevertheless, she was the only one I knew who could help.

"Althea, you were right. Something evil is stalking us. What should we do?"

Tony returned with a glass of water and she took a sip. "I need something stronger," she said. He did not argue, but hurried back to the kitchen.

"We've got to do a spell, right?" I asked.

Althea stared into space, thinking of one, I hoped.

"The liquid silver," I prompted. "You said if the beast swallowed the silver it would die and release the human. I lost the vial you gave me - do you have more?"

This jolted her from the zoned out state. Her beady eyes gazed bird-like at me. "Something else is in wolfen territory. There will be a great battle."

The change from a confident practitioner of magic arts to frightened old woman confounded me. Tony returned with a silver flask. She took it and sucked back a big gulp, like it was going to anchor her to safety.

Tony saw my expression and shrugged. "Vodka," he mouthed.

"You must stay out of the orchard at night." Her breathing and voice had returned to normal.

"What is it?" Impatience had crept into my voice.

Her eyes flashed anger. "No! Another creature is challenging the wolfen." She glanced toward the curtained window, as if expecting to see something terrifying.

"Then we really need to get going on this, Aunt Althea." I was trying to remain calm. With her experience in the supernatural, I wanted her to be the one with the answers. "Rob will be at our house Thursday night. When the moon is full."

"I can't think now," she said and pushed herself out of the chair. "You must not do anything more. Just stay locked in your house at night." She retreated from the room muttering, "I have to consult with my colleagues."

Neither Tony nor I spoke during the short drive home. He took the 3-minute drive down to the road and around to our driveway. When he pulled up in front of our door he turned to me.

"Are you okay?"

"I don't know."

In the dimness of the truck cab his dark eyes were soft. He could have said 'I told you she was nuts', but he didn't.

"She was really scared, Tony. Why? And why won't she help us if she's so worried about our safety?"

"Because she doesn't know what to do about the wolfen or other spooks anymore than you do."

"Ah ha!"

He put up a palm. "I don't believe in bogey beasts. I'm just saying...if there were such a thing, she wouldn't know what to do about it."

"What should I do?"

He reached across the seat and took my hand. "Let's start living in the real world. When I get home I'll call Nick. And I'll help you anyway I can."

I remembered holding his hand lots of times when we were little kids – wading in the creek below the hill, crossing the road to visit neighbors, when he helped me down from a tree. It always felt safe like this. I slowly pulled away, relishing the feel of his rough palm sliding against my skin.

I smiled, with all I felt for him probably right there in my eyes. "Thanks."

Chapter 24

Shannon's room reeked of minty foot lotion and the "French Quarter" red polish she had applied to her toenails. As I described to her the wolfen marks by the cabin she fastidiously wiped errant polish from around each toe with a cotton swab and indulged in a moment of admiration for her pretty feet. Then she looked me in the eye and – surprise, surprise – accused me of making things up. The word, "liar" rolled off her tongue, after which I endured more insults regarding my sanity.

When she waved her arm to emphasize a point about my obsessiveness, the watchband slipped up and down. From what I had learned in Althea's wolfen book – which was all I could rely on now - I knew I had to weaken Rob's hold over her. The fur band had to be destroyed.

After she went to bed around 11:30 I gave her another hour to make sure she was sleeping. While I waited, I reviewed the chapter that described the wolf hair belts werewolves use to slip in and out of beastliness. The directions on how to destroy the fur belt in order to weaken the beast were very specific, and I intended to follow them.

As soon as I detected her faint snore I crept into her room with a penlight and found the watch on her nightstand not far from her upturned face. The rough fur must have been irritating to her skin and I felt a twinge of regret for what I was about to do, considering how much the gift from Rob meant to her.

I almost put it back. Almost. I reminded myself she was under a spell and would thank me someday. Maybe when we reached our 80's.

While separating the watch from the band I padded quietly down the stairs, two flights, to the family room where I had prepared our big wood-burning fireplace, unused since winter with newspaper and kindling. Once lit, the fire took only seconds to consume the fur. As I watched, I imagined a wolfish face in the flames.

It took one minute for the room to fill with smoke and the foul odor of burning fur.

I struggled to open the chimney flue as the smoke grew thicker, but the iron latch stuck. By the time I managed to pull it out, my throat was burning. I fanned the air with a magazine from the fire starter pile but not soon enough to avoid setting off the smoke detector, which pierced the quiet of the house and soon brought Shannon downstairs. Looking disheveled and sour faced she quickly assessed my guilty expression and rushed to see what was in the fireplace. She made a move to retrieve the band, realized it was too late, and pulled back.

She turned on me and shouted over the din from the smoke detector. "You are deranged! What right do you think you have to steal something of mine and destroy it? You...you...I hate you!"

She shook as her eyes filled up with tears. "You should either be put in a facility for the insane or kept locked up here where you can become a kooky old spinster like Tony's aunt."

She glared at me for several long seconds.

"From now on, you are not to speak to me except when absolutely necessary. It's going to be a long time before I can forgive you, Raine." She left the room, giving me no time to reply. I felt every thump of her feet up the two flights of stairs back to her bedroom and winced when the door slammed.

"I'd rather be in an asylum than dating a werewolf," I shouted.

By then the watchband was just a small ember and although the room was hazy, most of the smoke had disappeared up the chimney. I got a pitcher of water from the kitchen and threw it over the hot ashes, watching the steam rise up after the smoke.

After a while, with everything under control I went out to the back yard and sat down on the deck. When Jake came to me I let him lick my face.

Chapter 25

S hannon didn't work on Sundays but she left the house early the next morning without telling me where she was going, no doubt to visit Rob. I hoped he didn't have another fur bracelet to give her because I couldn't do anything for her now except wait for the bonfire and full moon.

My friend Tia came by at 10 in her father's white convertible Mustang. Big sunglasses and dark hair in a casual pull back accentuated her fine-boned face and gave her a movie star glamor. She laughed when I asked to bring Jake to the beach, as if it was a joke.

"Jake needs to cool off too," I said.

"I don't want to mess up my Dad's car."

"I'll put a towel over the seat." I knew swimming was a good way to wear out a dog and I was becoming more attached to having Jake with me as often as possible.

Tia was usually a pretty good sport so she gave in, but kept checking Jake in the rear view window as she drove.

"When were you going to invite me to your bonfire?" she said after a while.

I gaped at her hoping I hadn't heard her correctly. Shannon had only been planning the party for a few days. How had my recluse sister managed to spread the word so quickly?

"It's all over social media. Did you think it was a secret?"

"I can't believe she did that. Imagine how many crazies are going to show up."

"Lots. So...am I invited or not?"

My mind turned slowly as I considered warning her of the danger. Thinking about the nature of our friendship I decided it would not weather a revelation like Rob the werewolf.

"Shannon has never thrown a party before and I'm worried it might be lame. I don't want to watch her embarrass herself. Why don't we do something else? How about that Zucchini Blossom Café again? We might meet some cool musicians."

She laughed. "Oh, it won't be lame. There's quite a buzz about the cool bonfire party in the orchard and everyone is going to be there – I wouldn't be surprised if some musicians show up too."

"This is not good," I murmured and slouched in the seat, defeated. "Obviously, you don't need an invitation from me."

"But it would have been nice to get one anyway."

"Tia, this might end up a disaster."

She laughed. "Summer bonfire, hundreds of unknown partiers and substances...what could go wrong?"

Great. Shannon had unwittingly arranged for a large audience to witness the transformation of the beast she was dating.

When we arrived at the lake the bright cloudless sky was heating the sand up fast while all the best spots for lying on towels were taken, so Tia and I found a less-than-perfect place close to the water and our backs to the people strolling by.

While Tia arranged her towel for maximum exposure, I threw a stick into the lake for Jake.

He plunged in without hesitation and brought the prize back to me with tail waving high. As soon as he dropped it he shook himself, earning squeals from Tia and me, which he assumed was praise, judging by his wagging tail. The second throw I heaved out as far as I could, and hit a one-man rubber dingy trailed by a paddling dog.

The guy snatched the stick and held it out for Jake to see, then threw it a few feet away. Both Jake and the other dog went after it while the young man paddled his dingy to shore.

He hopped out and pulled the craft up toward us with a friendly grin. It was Keith, the guy who had been sitting beside me during my one humiliating day of dog training.

"Hey! Raine."

I introduced him to Tia who gave him her brightest smile and he responded in kind.

While our dogs romped on shore, Keith plopped down in the sand beside Tia, and I took advantage of the opportunity to find out if I was the only person who thought Rob's training abilities sucked. "How is your dog doing? Are you getting a lot out of Alpha Guy's class?"

He shook his head. "You know, Rob is not nearly as harsh to the other dogs as he was to yours."

"That's what I thought. He's got a grudge against Jake. How weird is that?"

"Any idea why?" he asked.

"A couple of theories."

While the dogs played on shore he settled in for a long visit. "Are you going to that big bonfire party I hear is happening near Long Hill Road?"

Tia laughed while I tried not to look peeved. I mumbled "yes" and called for Jake. For the next hour I played with the dogs while Tia and Keith got to know each other.

Tia drove us home with a soft smile playing on her lips. When the car rolled up in front of my house she reached back and gave Jake a friendly pat.

"Great idea bringing the dog. Excellent guy bait."

I smiled as we got out but she noticed my mood was not as sunny as hers.

"What's wrong? You don't mind about Keith, do you?"

"No."

She gave me a teasing look. "Tony?"

I blushed. "No, I'm worried about someone showing up at the party and turning into a beast," I said.

She snorted. "I hope lots of beasts show up. It's summer – time to be wild."

Dear sweet innocent Tia.

"Not too wild," I said. "We still have to face my parents when they get home."

She laughed. "Call me later." Her car disappeared in the dust and with a surge of gas roared onto the main road. As I stood there thinking, Jake nudged me with a lick on my hand, which is dog speak for "Move".

I took extra time feeding him and brushing him before we left for my afternoon shift at the fruit stand – he now seemed to be the only friend I could really confide in. When we got home around 8 pm Shannon's bedroom door was closed, her favorite music blaring from within.

Chapter 26

Early the next morning the acrid stench of burnt pancakes and smoking bacon did not entice Shannon out of her bedroom, even to complain. I gave up trying to make them perfect after flipping 10, and scraped half into the garbage. The other half I gave to Jake who ate all the burnt bacon as well. I sipped a fruit smoothie until her door finally creaked open and she scooted down stairs past the kitchen and to the family room without looking my way, as if I was invisible. A moment later I heard the whir of the treadmill and the rhythmic pounding of her feet.

The doorbell snapped me out of my gloom. Jake ran ahead of me barking so I spent a few moments convincing him to sit properly before I opened the door.

"He sure sounds formidable on this side," Nick said, grinning. "Good idea, getting yourselves a big dog."

Jake put his head down for Nick to pet.

"He sure likes you and Tony," I said.

"I feel honored. From what I hear he can be selective."

"He's a good judge of character."

"Better to have a dog like this than one who is too friendly. At least you know he's got your back when someone with bad intentions is lurking around here," he said. Tony must have told him everything. If Nick thought I was crazy too, he was keeping it to himself.

"So Tony told you about the lamb and claw marks?" I said.

"Yes. I've been to the cabin and those marks are on two other trees. They look man-made to me, like with a hook or something. Fish and Wildlife said no bears have been reported in the valley for over a year, so whoever pinched the lamb feasibly made those marks. I can't offer a motive for any of it except that maybe someone is playing a prank. Or some new weird cult has moved into the area. In any case, you and Tony just keep an eye out and don't hesitate to call me if you see anything else."

He paused and the steady beat on the treadmill filled the silence.

"Is that all you've got?"

He offered an apologetic smile. "The warden I talked to said there have been sightings of a large bear north of here near the mountains, but those marks aren't from a bear."

"No." I felt letdown.

"Do you mind interrupting Shannon for a second?"

At least she would have to respond to a summons from a cop. I went downstairs and found her with air buds in her ears, zoning out to her music. She tried to ignore me but I pulled the plug on the machine, and before her scowl could erupt in a yell, told her about our visitor. Wordlessly, she wiped her face and pits with a towel hanging from one of the bars and hurried upstairs, taking the steps two at a time. I followed.

Nick greeted her with a big glad-to-see-you grin but her response was reserved, as if they were acquaintances rather than friends who grew up together. I didn't understand it at all.

"I heard about your bonfire plans," he said.

"Don't worry, officer. I have a permit, designated drivers lined up and I will make sure no minors – if there are any – will be drinking." She lobbed a nasty glower my way.

He didn't seem bothered by her shortness. "I still don't think it's a good idea."

"Are you going to be checking up on us?"

"I may cruise by to make sure you're all right."

I thanked him. "Midnight would be a good time," I said, earning another look from my sister.

Nick chuckled. Yeah, Tony had shared my fears with him, and I imagined them having a laugh at my expense, but he said nothing except, "See you ladies later," and left.

Once he was gone Shannon's little frown deepened, which she pinned on me before running upstairs to shower. By 8:30 she had left for work.

I made a phone call to the Alpha Guy Dog Obedience Training Center and when a woman answered I asked for Rob. She told me he had taken the day off due to a sudden bout of flu. This was the first good news I'd had in days because it meant the burning of his fur bracelet had indeed weakened the beast in him. The next step was to get some more colloidal silver.

Aunt Althea may have lost her will to continue this fight, but my personal stakes were too high for me to back down now since not only was Shannon on the verge of being turned into a werewolf, but it could happen in front of two hundred people.

Althea's book provided additional information regarding the colloidal silver - that it worked best if administered during a full moon and right before the creature began its transformation, around midnight. The bonfire party was the perfect place and time to pull off Shannon's rescue from Rob; and perhaps even Rob's deliverance from the beast.

I intended to keep my eye on him all night if necessary, but first I decided to study him further by reviewing the training day video which I had uploaded but never viewed.

As I pulled the digital file up on my computer, I heard Tony's motorcycle pull into the yard and I leaned out my window as he pulled off his helmet.

"Come on up. I'll show you the training video of Rob and Jake."

He jogged up the stairs about a minute later and stood just inside the doorway, patting Jake and surveying my girlie stuff with a bemused smile. He hadn't been here since we were in elementary school playing video games and I felt awkward.

"Er...have a seat." I pulled out my desk chair for him and sat opposite on my bed. He plunked down without a trace of shyness and stretched out his legs. "So Nick reported what he found?"

"Yes. He wasn't much help."

He let that hang there for a moment then he said, "When were you going to invite me to the bonfire?"

I couldn't meet his eyes. "Did Nick tell you?"

"Everybody knows. Except I would rather have heard it from you instead of from the girls on the baseball team."

I sighed. "You've got to know, this isn't going to be an ordinary party."

He raised his brow. "Really? How so?"

"I will be there to guard Shannon, whether she appreciates it or not."

"Are you kidding me?"

"No."

"Even Aunt Althea advised you to give up."

"I know. And I figured you would too."

"Not if I could talk you into just enjoying the party. Nick is going to swing by a couple of times. I'm pretty sure he'll notice if Rob changes into a werewolf."

I elbowed him in the shoulder. Then I bent over beside him to bring the video up on the computer monitor, trying not to inhale too deeply his scent of soap and the outdoors. It was a familiar smell but something was different.

"What are you wearing?" I asked abruptly.

He looked startled.

I realized I sounded ridiculous. "I mean that scent. New cologne or something?"

A knowing smile played on his lips. "Do you like it?"

I pointedly stared at the computer monitor. "It's okay."

"Cause I'm not wearing cologne."

My cheeks grew warm. "It must be the woodsy monitor cleaner."

I found the file I was looking for and clicked 'play'. The camera was on Jake first, and in the background Rob's voice said "Drop the leash."

As Jake reached the washtub I noticed a shadowy mass to the left behind Rob.

I knew it wasn't a corruption in the file because Jake looked toward the mass as he jumped.

"What the heck is that?" Tony said.

As we watched the mass moved directly behind Rob and surrounded him with a faint grey aura.

This was not a simple flaw on the recording. When Jake jumped back to the floor he turned his head to look at Rob. During the actual event I hadn't thought much about it but now I realized he was probably looking at the thing around Rob. As Jake returned to me the shadow faded and disappeared. Now I remembered that after Jake's performance the rotten egg/fart stink had dissipated.

Tony let out a quiet whistle. "Replay it," he said.

The thing was so obvious on the video, why hadn't I noticed it while I was there?

Tony swiveled the chair around to face me. "The file must be corrupted."

"But you saw Jake look at the...thing."

He had no counter argument for that. "Are you going to show it to Shannon?"

"I'll try. But right now I want to show it to your aunt."

"What good would that do?"

"She knows what's going on."

"I'm not so sure about that."

"Yes, she does. That's why the claw marks rattled her. She must know something about this."

He took me back to his house and pulled up the video I'd emailed him on his laptop. We found his aunt reading a book in the shade of the umbrella on the patio, a pitcher of ice water and a glass on the table. Tony set the laptop in front of her.

I watched it from behind her for the fourth time, still expecting the dark form to not be there, like a mirage that disappears when the sun changes. But it was there. We both watched her face.

At first she closed her eyes and said nothing. Then she crossed herself. "Not good," she whispered.

"You said the man called to the spirit of the wolfen with his bracelet. Is this it?"

She closed her eyes again. After a moment Tony grew impatient.

"What is this thing?" he asked.

She looked up at him. "Powerful evil."

"So we are in danger," I said.

She stood up. "Yes, you are. Now I must talk to my friends. Then I can tell you more." She slowly made her way into the house.

Tony took me home. At first neither of us spoke, both trying to make sense of everything. I thought about calling my parents but what could they do in Greece besides worry? Or worse, think I was losing my mind and blame Tony's aunt. He turned to me as his truck rolled to a stop in front of our house.

"She's a smart girl," he said. "Maybe your disapproval is driving her to Rob. Maybe if you pulled back things would work out better."

I needed that advice a few days ago. Now, it was too late. The wolf was at the door and I had to stand guard.

He reached out to stroke my hand.

"Aunt Althea will come up with something," he assured me, but neither of us believed it. She had clearly been upset.

I found Shannon sunning herself in the backyard in a bikini. I didn't even know she had a bikini - she was pale but she looked good in it.

Jake, who had been lying in the shade of one of Mom's plum trees trotted over to greet me. "Hey, buddy! You'd better let Shannon have some of your shade. She's getting kinda pink."

She glared at me. "Just so there's no misunderstanding, I am never going to forgive you for burning my watchband."

"You need to watch the video I took of Jake on our first training day. It shows..."

"Give it up! I'm sick of you."

"But..."

She put her hand out as if warding off a blow. I stared at her a moment but she wouldn't look at me. I took Jake and went to my bedroom where I changed into my bikini. I sunned myself on my parents' balcony and let her pretend I didn't exist. I wished I could do the same thing about Rob.

Chapter 27

Shannon managed to avoid me Tuesday and Wednesday so when I wasn't working, Jake and I practiced his obedience commands, which he now performed consistently well – flawlessly, even. At least she could not accuse the dog or me of not holding up our end of the training bargain.

On Wednesday evening I attended a baseball game between Nick and Tony's team, the Crazy Cadillacs, and an out of town team. Tia played third base, having signed on, like many of the girls, because Nick Callus coached. I couldn't play this season as my shift at the fruit stand included some afternoons and weekends, but I tried to lend cheering support whenever possible.

This evening the CC's won 8-3 and Tony invited me to join them for a victory pizza. The girls pulled together enough tables to seat everyone around, and sandwiched me between Tia and the first basewoman, while Tony and the female assistant coach sat across from us. Tony and I didn't have much of a chance to talk but I liked the way his eyes kept sliding to mine, like we shared a secret language. It was new, yet not.

Nick held court at the end of the table enjoying the attention of his players, some of whom also indulged in a little flirting. To me, his grin seemed a bit wolfish which made me blink hard to clear my mind from images of werewolves everywhere. I turned away and caught Tony unabashedly starring at me with a faint smile. Could he tell I felt like I was losing my mind?

He gave Tia and me a ride home in his pick-up truck, with me sitting next to him, aware of his thigh against mine. After he dropped her off I started to slide over but he stopped me with his hand on my knee. "Why don't you stay where you are?"

We didn't talk much the rest of the way home but our bodies were communicating. I felt like I had a fever and when the truck stopped in front of my house I quickly scooted out.

"Thanks for the ride," I said.

"You're welcome, Raine," he said softly before I closed the door.

By 8 a.m. on Thursday morning Shannon was outside loading apple boxes on a flat, which she towed with Dad's ATV out to the fire pit. The pit nestled in a grove of overgrown cherry trees on the opposite side of our house to the Callas property, only viewable from the upstairs deck.

I joined her while she was arranging the boxes as benches around the grove, and offered to help, but she refused to acknowledge me. I tried not to let it get to me and left her alone. She's gotta wake up some time, I told myself.

From the deck I watched her haul firewood and old crate slats to the pit. Once everything was in place she followed the rough trail to the main road where she put up a crude cardboard sign that said: "HERE". Did she have a clue how many people were planning to swarm her party?

Later in the afternoon I found her talking on her cell phone in the kitchen. As soon as she saw me, she signed off.

"Who was that?" I asked.

She appeared conflicted between talking or not. At last her need to punish won and she said, "BTW. If you plan on hanging around when my friends are here, you'd better not cause any trouble."

"What friends? People are coming because of a bonfire party in an orchard. They don't care who is having it."

She glared. I'd hit a nerve. I pushed: "Are you even sure Rob is coming?"

"Why wouldn't he?"

"I dunno. He might break up with you." I didn't want Shannon to be embarrassed – okay, maybe a little. But mostly I wanted Rob to move on and leave her as a human. Even the irritable human she had become.

She mustered up an arrogant laugh. "FYI, that was him on the phone, checking to make sure the party is still on. He is SMTM."

"What do those letters stand for?"

"Smitten. Will you be in attendance?" Her expression said she would rather have a rodent show up than me.

"Of course. But I'll deny I had anything to do with it if Mom and Dad find out."

She laughed again, more haughtily.

I shook my head at how silly she had become. "BTW. You've lost your brains over beast boy." Yeah, that was mature.

Althea hadn't yet contacted me with more information on Rob's shadowy Thing, so I decided another visit was required. Three magpies perched on the roof just above the door of the Callus house and squawked, one at a time, in short conversational bursts. "Friends of Althea's?" I said and laughed. I swear they all laughed back.

"Tony is not here," Althea said through the 4-inch crack of the door.

I was determined to get some answers and so I more or less pushed my way in. Her skin was pale and her eyes pinched as she backed away and retreated to her wingback chair in the living room. Jake did not try to win a pat from her but stayed by the door, as if he knew we would not be long.

"I have no more information regarding this dog trainer," she said.

"The party is tonight. You said we were in danger. What do you think is going to happen?"

When she didn't answer I added more sharply, "I need to be prepared."

"This is not a fight for children. Stay home."

"I'm not a child and my sister thinks she's in love with Rob. I need to help her. Is he a werewolf? Was that shadow in the video the spirit of the werewolf? Or a regular ghost?"

She put her hands together as if in supplication and closed her eyes until the central air conditioner kicked in with a low rumble causing her to jump. She made an air sign of the cross.

My watch showed 7 pm and I wanted to get home to shower and change in time for the party but I waited her out.

"Come." She hoisted herself from the chair and I followed her to the kitchen where she rummaged around in a drawer. When she found what she was looking for she handed it to me - a large spray can. Bear spray.

"Really?"

She nodded solemnly. "Even the eyes and sinuses of a shape shifter cannot withstand pepper spray."

I read the instructions, which indicated the beast had to be too close for my comfort in order for the spray to stop him. I said so.

She sighed and looked away. "There may be one more action you can do - a difficult thing but it could work if you understand it."

"Anything."

She left the kitchen and came back a few minutes later with a large, leather bound book and held it out to me. It was a Bible.

"Book of advanced spells," she explained.

She pushed it into my hands leaving me no choice but to grab it. "Take it to the party. When the demon wolf manifests itself, spray him, then hold the Bible up. It might scare him."

"What if it doesn't?" I tried to hand it back. "What about the other stuff you told me?"

She gestured impatiently and leaned forward with an unblinking gaze. "No man or woman can know all the forms evil takes. My knowledge is small and my potions are few, handed down for centuries,

but how or why they work..." she shrugged. "This darkness in the video
– stronger than my little herbal bags."

At last, an honest admission. I didn't know what to say. After being
strung along with her potions and incantations, I felt her honesty was
too little too late. Indignation rose inside me. "Maybe if all else fails I
can whack Rob with it. But I'm going to look weird bringing a Bible."

She nodded her approval. "Believe me, if your dog trainer is
possessed, no one will notice you."

As I was leaving she called out after me, "But use the pepper spray
first."

"SO THIS IS WHAT A WEREWOLF slayer wears these days," Tony
said. He stood on the doorstep, himself in mid-calf shorts and a black
t-shirt. I wasn't wearing anything special, just the basic summer
uniform of shorts and a sleeveless blouse, but I smiled at his approval
anyway.

"I heard you were at the house today," he said.

He followed me inside as I told him about my visit with Althea,
including her advice to use the combination pepper spray and the giant
Bible to whack it in the head after it was immobilized by the spray.

He laughed. "I didn't know she had a Bible."

"I guess I'll try the bear repellant first."

"You're actually going to spray your sister's boyfriend with pepper
spray?"

I checked the contents of the backpack - which included the heavy
Bible - and set it by the door. "Maybe the werewolf won't show up...but
Shannon plans to lose her virginity to this guy. Pepper spray will come
in handy then too."

His eyes widened.

I grinned at him. "The trouble is, I have to get very close to be
accurate, like this." I moved very close and smiled into his eyes while

holding an invisible can above my head. He stared back for one heartbeat then took hold of my arm and pulled me close. I lost my ability to breath. His voice was low and husky. "Just don't spray me when I try to kiss you, okay?"

I gasped and he stepped back. A smile of victory played on his lips, leaving my thoughts unsteady and knees confused...or was that thoughts confused and knees unsteady? "I won't..."

An awkward silence stretched between us before he turned me toward the door. "We are going to have fun for a while before you swing into battle, okay?"

Chapter 28

The relentless bass penetrated the entire orchard while the flash of flames, noisy laughter, and smell of smoke and burning hot dogs drew us in as we walked across the orchard.

"Raine, you should try not to be too obvious when you're watching Rob and Shannon. Pretend you're more interested in me."

I gave him a sideways glance. "That might work."

On Shannon's orders I had left Jake in my bedroom to prevent him from ruining the party by "trying to eat the hotdogs or jumping on someone and pushing them into the fire". I did not argue with her. The book warned that fully formed werewolves easily destroyed dogs, and I wanted Jake to be safe.

"My first bonfire bash is going to be ruined because of Shannon's bad date choice," I grumbled.

Tony took my hand and replied with mock solemnness. "We can have fun while it lasts."

As we approached, many more people were arriving via the dirt trail off the road where Shannon's sign beckoned, and several vehicles lined up beside the trail. Near the bonfire I counted about 40 guests, not many of whom I recognized. Some couples sat on apple boxes, fusing their bodies and lips together. Others talked, and still others burned marshmallows and hot dogs in the flames. A few hoisted beers in the air as they danced.

"This is as bad as I feared," I whispered as we entered the clearing. "Too many people."

"Don't worry," Tony said. "Nick will be swinging by, remember?" His eyes were bright with anticipation of a great party, and so I decided for his sake I should try to be more positive. Besides, I did like the way he stroked the back of my hand with his thumb.

Tia and Keith broke off from a group and greeted us. At the same time I spotted Shannon and Rob hunched together on a box. So their relationship had advanced to the point where she needed to be caressing his arm or leg. Yet he leaned into her without touching. Was it because he felt awkward with a human female?

Tia followed my gaze. "Pretty weird, Shannon with a boyfriend. I never thought it would happen in my lifetime. Great makeover."

"She is as deserving of a boyfriend as anyone," I said. "It just shouldn't be Rob."

Keith snorted. "She sure seems stuck to Alpha Guy."

Shannon's fawning over Rob made me embarrassed for her. She behaved like a woman who had recently been released from science prison into the land of hormones.

I felt a squeeze on my hand. Tony's eyes, watching me so intensely, reflected the fire. I leaned my face to his shoulder and his arm pressed me closer, erasing all thoughts of Shannon. The cobalt sky was lit by a bright full moon and a gazillion stars.

Soon, every person was moving – dancing to the music, undulating in an embrace, or sneaking away to pee in the dark. The restlessness seemed to collect over us and develop its own personality.

Keith and Tia eventually drifted away to talk to others. Tony pulled up a box for us to sit on and I found myself leaning into him, like the other couples. I shook my head to his offer of food and drink, not wanting him to move.

My phone, wedged in the pocket of my jeans, signaled a text message from Dad: "Zoom in 30 min. Important." I told Tony.

"Don't let this bug you now. They want to tell you abut their trip so far, i'm sure. I'll go up to the house with you."

I figured they somehow found out about the party. Maybe Aunt Althea had called Tony's parents. Of course, they would not suspect Shannon had anything to do with it, which is why they wanted to talk to me.

Tony gave a light tug on my arm. "Want to dance?"

A few people moved around the fire to the beat of the music, not avoiding bumping into others trying to roast wieners, but so far no one had fallen in. Tony drew me closer to the dark edge of the grove.

When the booming music ended a gap of silence dragged by. A few protested while Rob checked the pod on the speaker dock. Before he could get it restarted a police siren shrieked not far away, and continued into the distance for a few moments until our music exploded into the chords of an old song I'd heard on 'classic radio', "Born to be Wild", obliterating the siren. The scenario heightened the wanton mood of the partiers and they began dancing as one crazy mindless entity.

I shuddered.

Keith, dancing with Tia a few feet away from us, stopped moving and craned his neck up to the sky to let go of an inhuman howl. Soon most of the other guys joined in, as well as some of the girls – indulging in deranged eerie baying at the moon.

A cold finger lifted the hair on my neck as I distinguished one unique cry amongst all the others, more like a voice of despair than a celebration. I knew it had to be Rob, whose head was back, howling in a tone and cadence so different from the others. No one else, including Shannon and Tony, seemed aware of his weird lamentation.

I couldn't tear my gaze away from Rob, expecting his face to transform at any moment as the din carried on and on until people's throats were sore.

As Tony took a big drink from his juice bottle I elbowed him, causing some juice to spill.

"What...?" he sputtered.

"Didn't you hear that?"

"The howling? Yes."

"Rob's howling. Like a wounded animal. Couldn't you hear it?"

"Separate from all the others? No."

"He was calling to the evil forces."

"Are you kidding?"

"No! The pitch was too distinctive."

Why couldn't anyone else discern the truth about Rob?

I glanced again at what was now an empty space and clutched Tony's arm. "Where did they go?"

"Calm down. I saw them leave. They probably want to make out away from the fire."

That possibility did not calm me down. "Do you have any idea what he can do to her in the dark while they make out? She may come back with long teeth and fur all over herself."

Tony shook his head. "We don't think that anymore, do we?"

As my eyes scanned the shadows I saw movement and something big, dark and furry flashed just outside the grove.

Tia, who was standing over on that side of the fire, jumped and peered into the dark.

"Did you see that?" I asked Tony.

"Yes." He frowned.

"It was too big to be a dog and not human – unless someone is messing with us." I took a step forward with the intention of trying to detect more, but he stopped me.

"We should stay right where we are."

Lowell, a former lab partner of Shannon's, stood not far from us with an unlit cigar dangling from his fingers and telltale marshmallow cream on his upper lip.

"Hey, I saw some eyes out there," he said, peering into the dark.

"Quit messing around, Lowell." Keith said. "Nobody believes a guy with marshmallow on his face."

"No, really. Two red eyes, like a devil beast or something." Lowell gave a little nervous laugh.

This could be the showdown and I was not as ready as I thought; in fact, I couldn't seem to remember what I was supposed to do. Tony swallowed, also peering in the same direction as Lowell. We were both rooted to our spots, waiting for something bad to happen while everyone else except for Lowell partied on, unaware of the impending catastrophe.

Shannon and Rob stepped into the firelight a few feet left of the sighting, startling us. Lowell laughed with hearty relief and raised his cigar. "Hey, we thought you were a bear. Where have you been?"

"We are not about to share our secrets," Shannon replied coyly, not once looking at me.

Lowell shrugged and as he drifted toward another group Rob's eyes met mine with an expression of smugness, like he had won first prize. My heart sank.

"Something's happened between those two," I said to Tony. "He's been too busy...do you think he brought his wolf?"

"Why don't we ask them?" Before I could protest, he strode over to Shannon and Rob pulling me along.

"Did you bring your wolf?" He raised his voice to be heard over the music.

Rob looked like a dope caught in the headlights of a car before he slid a glance toward Shannon. When she gave a slight shake he relaxed. "I don't know what you are talking about."

She must have been too embarrassed to tell him about my visit to his wolf shed.

"We glimpsed something outside the grove that looked like a wolf. Lowell did too. Look, he's bailing cause he's scared."

Lowell had just thrown his cigar into the fire and was exiting the grove in the opposite direction from where we witnessed the animal.

I persisted. "We need to alert everyone and let them decide if they want to stay or not."

Shannon's eyes narrowed. "I warned you about ruining my party."

"I saw it too," Tony said. "It may be a bear if not a wolf. Either one would crash and ruin your party."

"Bears don't come down to the valley until fall and they rarely get this close to a fire and a bunch of people. If Raine is scared why don't you take her back to the house?"

Humiliation inflamed my cheeks and I bit my lip, too hurt to think of a come back.

I heard Tony mutter under his breath. Without warning he jumped up on one of the apple crates and called out to get everyone's attention. "A few of us have seen something out there. We think it might be a bear."

Not everyone could hear him over the music but those closest just stared, until one of the guys jumped up on another apple crate, waved his bottle of coke and started grunting in a dopey imitation of a bear.

That was all it took to get a couple of laughs from the hyped up crowd. I knew no one wanted to be labeled a baby by leaving early, especially since there might be a great morning-after story brewing. Someone else growled, a girl squealed, more laughter, and everyone turned back to whatever they were doing, including those making out.

Tony jumped off the crate.

I threw my arms around him. "Thanks for trying."

He didn't let me pull away as fast as I intended and spoke into my ear, his breath warm and intimate. "Let's go back to the house and wait for your call. We'll be back before midnight."

But I had one more thing to say to my sister. "I've never done anything to be mean, Shannon, only to save you from *him*. Remember that when things start to happen."

Stone-faced, she turned away.

Tony took my hand. "Come on. We need to get out of this smoke for a while."

Chapter 29

We hurried along the path followed by faint shadows that moved with the fluttering of leaves. A large form broke away and flew silently ahead of us, then dived behind a tree like a stealth bomber, talons crushing a squeak from its prey.

Tony whistled a thin reedy tune along with the music from the party, possibly thinking the noise would calm us, but instead creeped me out even more.

I stopped to dig the pepper spray from my fanny pack and handed it to him, which he took without hesitation.

"I wonder when Nick is going to show up," I said, trying not to shake.

"If he's occupied somewhere else he might be a while." A flash of worry crossed his face in spite of his effort to hide it from me.

"Do you mind if we run?" I asked.

"No."

He could have out run me but he didn't and I kept pace with him as we raced between two rows, the gloom nipping at our sanity. Once inside the house I dead-bolted the door. The wall clock in the kitchen ticked louder than usual as we waited and calmed our breathing.

We agreed Tony would not be included in the call, so as not to arouse further suspicion from my parents regarding our late night activities, and I attempted to suppress my guilt. Nevertheless I jumped when the computer phone rang at exactly 11p.m.

Dad's face popped up on the monitor, his expression stiff with concern. "Honey, how are things going?"

"Things are great. The apples look great, we've been doing our chores, and I'm enjoying my job. The Abels are still pregnant but ready to pop, and my dog is learning new tricks."

He ignored my babbling. "Angelo got a call from Althea. She told him you found gouges on a tree by the cabin and she is quite stressed about it. She thinks a bear is stalking the farms."

She must have said "bear" to avoid a brush-off.

"I explained I had arranged for the tree removal service to take the dead trees up there. Someone must have marked them for the diggers next week. I don't think she believed me. She insisted I phone and tell you to stay out of the orchard."

"Tree service?"

"I'm surprised you didn't notice the two other dead trees with the same marks. I'm sorry I forgot to mention it."

For a moment I thought he must be mistaken – those gouges were just like the wolfen sign in the book. I almost didn't believe him.

"I hope I didn't cause you too much worry," he said.

"I knew they weren't bear marks."

"Good. You and Shannon getting along?"

"Sure."

Thankfully the conversation ended soon since Mom was sleeping and Dad didn't want to wake her. After I said goodbye and shut the computer, Tony couldn't resist adding, "And we can expect a logical explanation for everything else, too."

I allowed him his moment of celebration before reminding him of the thing on the video, AND pointed out we had no reasonable explanation for the misplaced lamb.

"Come to think of it, Dad didn't mention your sheep. I wonder why Althea didn't tell them?"

"She is kind and doesn't want my parents to think I haven't been doing my job." He folded his arms. "I repeat, there are logical explanations for EVERYTHING."

The wheels turning in his "logical" mind kept him silent until he had another light bulb moment.

"Maybe Rob is one of those guys who likes a good joke."

"He doesn't have a sense of humor, believe me."

"You've been so focused on this werewolf idea of yours that you missed a lot of normal stuff. For instance, he likes wolves, right? Maybe he and Shannon planned this as a theme party - I wouldn't be surprised if at midnight somebody in an ugly wolf costume roars out of the bushes and scares the sh... out of everybody."

He had skirted the issue of the video. I checked my watch. 11:19.

"I agree with you, something is going to happen at midnight, for sure. Now let's check on Jake."

Tony followed me upstairs and was right behind me when I opened the door to a deserted room.

We both did a frantic search of the house and back yard while I called to him, even after I knew he couldn't be anywhere close by. We ended up in the kitchen, where the clock ticked "Emp-ty, emp-ty, emp-ty" and I didn't know what else to do.

"He's gone."

Tony shook his head. "Remember how he scaled the fence in your yard? I bet Rob and Shannon were up here during the time they went missing from the party, and put him in the back yard. Then, Jake probably jumped the fence to look for you. He wouldn't go far. In fact, maybe the flash of fur by the bonfire was him."

"He would have come to me."

"Maybe not. He's not used to parties with all the noise and people. Come on, let's go look for him."

He seemed pleased he had figured out another logical explanation for a mysterious event and in this case I wanted to believe him. I secured all my wolfen supplies in the fanny pack, found two flashlights, and followed Tony back out into the night.

Chapter 30

As we made our way back to the grove, we swept the area ahead with the beam of our flashlights and called out for Jake, even though I had faint hope he would hear us if he was anywhere near the noisy party.

With our approach the music got louder and the smoke heavier. Tia and Keith emerged from the smoky light and approached us.

"Hey, where have you two been?" Instead of the usual tease Keith appeared uneasy. "We've been hearing grunting noises coming from outside the grove and people are leaving. Tia is afraid to walk down to the car so would you mind lighting the way?"

She trembled a little in spite of the warm night. "We're pretty sure it's a bear and I want to get out of here. Too bad it's ruining Shannon's great party." Her smile was apologetic.

"A flashlight won't save us from a bear," I pointed out.

Tia nodded her head. "Oh yeah. Just shine the light in his eyes while we all run to the car."

I wondered how safe she thought the holder of the flashlight would be?

"Have you seen my dog?"

They hadn't.

"Has Rob been around?" Tony asked, still thinking Rob was a prankster.

"Off and on," Keith said.

Tia demanded they get going so Tony accompanied them to their car while I continued on to the grove.

I wasn't scared for Tony because no bear lurked in the orchard. We faced something supernatural and as midnight fast approached I feared for Shannon.

I also pushed aside my concern for Jake and instead concentrated on a battle plan.

Three more party deserters passed me heading for the light from Tony's flashlight. Only seven people besides Shannon and Rob remained by the time I entered the grove. Three were dancing, one couple was making out, and the Cooper sisters were charcoaling marshmallows. Someone had been keeping the bonfire well fueled and so the flames would continue to lick at the moon for a while yet.

A curtain of shimmering heat waves and smoke obscured Shannon's ability to see me. She peered into the dark until Rob loomed up behind her and slobbered on her neck. I crept closer to hear him tell her not to worry – if everyone left he could still give her a night to remember.

Gag.

A little frown creased her brow. "It's too early. Raine is so dead."

Afraid he would bite her and thus infect her with his saliva, I rushed into the light. "Get your paws off her, Rob."

Shannon stiffened. "How dare you? After ruining my party with your stupid prank." Her voice was louder than necessary and the others turned our way. She blamed me for the animal noises in the dark, and with that realization I formed a plan to get her away from Rob. I strode over to the speakers and killed the music.

"Jake is missing. I need you to help me look for him."

The fire cracked and sprayed embers and ashes while Shannon regarded me with stony eyes. "Set your mind at rest. He's safe and sound in the back of Rob's SUV."

It was the last thing I expected. "Where did you find him?"

"I sold him to Rob. For the $150 you owe me for dog training lessons."

My relief quickly drained away as fast as it had come.

She continued: "Since you burned my property without my permission you need a lesson in how it feels to lose something you value."

Despair threatened to choke me. "You can't sell him. He's my dog!" I cried.

"Really? When you brought him home you said he was our dog – for protection. Well we don't need protection. I've got Rob." She beamed at her prize, and he grinned back, the tips of his canine teeth sharp like a predator's.

"He doesn't cause any trouble."

Rob gave a short mean laugh. "He lunged at me again when we went into the house. You haven't made any headway with him at all."

In my peripheral vision I saw the smoke form a wolf's head near his face, but when I looked straight on, it disappeared. I checked my watch – 11:50. I cast another side glance toward him but this time discerned nothing.

"You've locked him up so he can't stop you." I took two slow breaths to ban the fear from my mind and remember what I must do. Slowly I reached inside the fanny pack for the bear spray while I watched for signs of his transformation, scanning with my eyes every inch of him as he pulled back his lips in an ugly snarl.

Finally, my eyes alighted on his feet. This night he wore sandals rather than boots - perhaps because his feet expanded when he changed form – exposing uncommonly ugly feet tufted with thick hair, and capped by long toenails.

What does one say to a guy about to transform into a wolf?

"My, what big toenails you have."

The Cooper sisters laughed, and another couple scurried away.

"Time for you to leave," Shannon snapped at me.

Rob said nothing, unblinking eyes on me. I was sure he could smell my fear, maybe even feel my trembling. The lift of his chin told me he believed he had won, which was okay, because I needed to lull him into a false sense of security.

"And what a big muzzle you have."

"Raine, shut up." Anger gave her voice a throaty timbre, like a she-wolf, but I couldn't take my eyes off Rob, who shifted into his loose hip stance, hands on hips.

"I think your sister is losing it." His curled lip exposed a long canine tooth.

"And what big teeth you have."

"You are certifiably insane." Shannon's voice was rising.

Out beyond the light in the grove, something snorted, causing me to jump. Neither Rob nor Shannon reacted, perhaps too far away from the sound.

I willed myself not to run and met his eyes full on. "What's out there? Your familiar?"

The moon reflected in his large black pupils. "Do you have a clue what you're saying?"

A branch snapped close by.

"It's still out there," one of the Cooper sisters said. At last the two of them and the rest of the guests scrambled away in the direction toward the cars. We three were left alone. Perhaps it was best.

"I understand your pain, Rob." I spoke in a soothing tone. "You can't control the wolf inside, can you? I'm here to help you. Send your familiar away."

"Shut up, you idiot," Shannon said.

I ignored her and kept my eyes on the shifting shadows of his face. "Rob, trust me. You don't have to change into a werewolf. I know the words to banish the demon."

He laughed. "Is this because of the dog?"

My hand tightened around the spray can. I expected to use it as soon as he let his guard down or the thing in the orchard attacked me – whichever came first.

His expression changed from amusement to contempt. "Jake is no ordinary dog. He's wasted on you. I have big plans for him."

"Are you going to kill him?"

"Train him, you silly girl," Shannon said.

I saw the glint of crazy in his eyes. "He's going to kill him, Shannon. Jake is a wolfen killer."

"A what!?"

I had read it in Althea's book, a small reference to a mysterious hound that showed up when a wolfen was about and made the wolfen disappear. The ancient writer did not know if the hound killed the beast or was able to banish it back to the portal of the supernatural.

Rob chuckled. "I saw that dog with the bottle picker and offered to buy him. The stupid old man told me the dog was meant for someone else. Where he found a Caelum Wolfhound I can't imagine since they're believed to be extinct. I offered him five thousand dollars but he turned his back on me and walked away. I couldn't find him or the dog again. Then you show up at my training center with him."

He shook his head. "Unbelievable! Some random girl who has no idea what she has, training him to do silly tricks.

"I can start a breeding program with Jake and my female wolf –the two of them will create a hybrid - thousands of dollars for one puppy. And the breed will be named after me – the Winslow Wolfhound."

In spite of his confession to being nothing more than a conniving dog breeder, I held onto the spray can, not sure what to do next. I wanted Jake back but whatever Shannon thought about Rob right now, there was no remorse or apology in the high tilt of her chin. We had had many spats over the years but I never felt this alienated from her.

And the matter of the shadow in the video had not been cleared up, nor that strange smoke formation I had just witnessed.

"I want my dog back."

"I'm afraid that's not possible. I'm going home." He started walking away.

"Now look what you've done." She followed after him. "Why don't we go up to the house?"

He shrugged her off in an unkind manner. "Sweetest Shannon, it's always been about the dog."

"What do you mean?"

He stopped. "Nothing personal. You're just not my type." He cast a contemptuous look at her hair. "I'm not into redheads."

The surprise and confusion on her face hurt me as much as the possibility of losing my dog.

"You're as evil as any werewolf," I flung at him.

He laughed. "I knew you were crazy the moment I saw you. It was easy to play all of you."

"You skulked around our orchard to see Jake the night after we met, didn't you? Your wolf howled."

He shrugged.

In the new light of his humanness I thought about everything that had happened. If he wanted the dog rather than a mate his bizarre training methods made sense - he was trying to make Jake unmanageable so he could get him away from me.

"Why the buried fur and the stolen lamb?" I said.

"I don't know what you're talking about." He started walking again.

Shannon grabbed his arm. "You were dating me to get the dog?"

He shook her off. "You handed him over so easily, I know I could have had him for free – and anything else too." His eyes mocked her – human mocking.

She stared at him for the longest time as if trying to make sense of his betrayal.

Then the brush rustled outside the grove nearest me.

"It's about time, Tony. What's taken you so long?" I said.

The answer was an animal-like noise. A grunting, non-dog noise.

Chapter 31

F ear shook all thought of werewolves from my mind. I had seen enough bears at zoos and on TV to know what one sounded like. I also knew from kids' survival camp that a person should never try to run from a bear, and I stayed frozen in my spot while trying to alert Shannon and Rob to the danger.

That's when I discovered it is impossible to yell without moving any part of the body. "Bear. Bear. Bear," I rasped.

They finally stopped arguing and looked my way, annoyance on both faces. Rob opened his mouth, no doubt to scold, but looked past me and stopped. Shannon's face went white. I turned slowly around as a big black bear ambled into the clearing and approached me. My body petrified into rock solid terror. The beast extended its snout and tested the air about five feet from my face and I closed my eyes in silent prayer. *God, Please don't let it eat me.* When I opened them again, the animal was still there. The odor its breath gave off was essence of rotting stomach contents but I managed not to twitch, hoping it would back off long enough for me to take the bear spray out of my fanny pack.

"Raine, don't move," Shannon said. Her voice was a loud whisper, as if she thought only I would be able to hear her.

Her warning was abruptly cut off by a tortured moan, which filled the night as it rose in pitch and volume. It wasn't coming from the bear, but I recognized it immediately, the other-worldly cry I'd heard from inside Alpha guy Dog Training Center on registration day.

The chilling noise distracted the bear and the beast turned away from me. I saw Rob loping like a dog toward the only jack pine amongst the cherry trees, his face twisted and mouth open. The inhuman noise was coming from him.

The bear took after him, a blur of fur shimmering in the firelight. Rob was faster, inhumanly fast. He shimmied up the skinny tree like a born climber with too-long arms. When he reached a limb at least 15 feet off the ground, he looked down at the bear and snarled like a wolf. I blinked. His canine teeth were now elongated fangs.

The bear stood and reached up with one front leg clawing at air inches below Rob's dangling leg, then pushed the thin trunk with both front paws. Rob hung on and snarled like a diesel engine. But instead of diesel I smelled rotten eggs.

The sound startled the bear and it thudded down on fours, growling in return.

A log in the fire exploded then the scent of the open bag of hot dogs must have called to him and he turned toward it.

A trickle of sweat down the back of my neck thawed my brain. I thought about escaping and readied the spray can toward the 400-lb beast now picking through the wrappings and lapping up all the remaining meat and buns.

Shannon moved slowly toward me. "You go!" she hissed, and gave me a push toward the darkness beyond the firelight. Her eyes darted nervously toward the bear and I knew she was planning to distract it. I shook my head and tried to motion her to go – my intention to follow her - when the bear interrupted me with a loud grunt. It was looking right at us, as if reconsidering our value to its feeding program. Bears have an amazing sense of smell, which wasn't good for us, since even I could smell the bucket of cologne Shannon had on. My finger tightened on the trigger of the bear spray.

Another log exploded, spraying burning embers several feet into the air. The bear bellowed and shook its head. I knew this wasn't a good time to cry and make noise but the tears were spilling out and I couldn't stop them. "I love you Shannon," I sniffed.

"Be quiet," she whispered back.

Rob must have figured out what I was holding and he started yelling from his perch. "Don't just stand there you dope! Spray him! Spray him!"

This reminded the bear that it was mad at Rob. It headed back to the tree and rising up, tried again to reach his leg. As Shannon and I watched, Rob's facial features darkened and became even more wolfish. He threw back his head, his mouth opened wide, and let out another deep gowl.

The bear answered with a louder bellow. It pushed its front legs against the trunk of the tree bending it back like it was made of rubber, bouncing parallel to the ground. Rob clung to the bucking branch with both arms, again answering the bear's roar with his own. I figured he didn't have long in this world, and neither did Shannon and I when the bear was finished with him.

Shannon tugged at my arm. "Now's our chance."

While I geared up the courage to move, in the distance I recognized Jake's distinct deep 'woof'. It came from somewhere down the trail to the main road and it was growing louder. What a beautiful sound.

The bear let go of the tree to sniff the air.

Jake's barking became more frantic as he approached and lunged into the clearing, leash dragging. Without hesitation he charged the bear with a ferocity and courage that transformed him – not my Jakey Wakey.

He was a blur of grey fur as he feinted from one side to the other. The bigger animal roared and took a swipe at him, but Jake dodged out of the way with ease, as if he had done this before. Then he lunged again, and again, cranking up the bear's agitation.

Tony materialized beside me. "Thank God. Come on." He pulled at me but I resisted. "No, Jake needs my help."

"No he doesn't," Shannon hissed.

"I think he's enjoying it," Tony said.

He was right. The bear hadn't been able to land a hit on him yet, and Jake seemed to be purposely drawing it away from the clearing as he continued to snap forward and pull back. After a minute they disappeared into the dark, thrashing about out of range of the light from the fire. I listen for a telltale yelp or squeal from my dog but it never came.

At last there was a final roar from the bear and the dull thud and crash of the animal fleeing and Jake's deep bark. For a moment neither Shannon nor I moved as the fire cackled and volleyed burning embers into the night.

A victory whoop drew our attention back to Rob who looked as if he had survived his bone-jarring experience without injury. He scrambled partway down and jumped, landing lightly on the ground. Then he shook himself like a wet dog.

The strange dark visage was gone and so were the long fangs. Nor did he appear to have any lingering trauma like I was feeling.

"What a great dog!" he said.

"You ran up the tree and left the women to fend for themselves," Tony said.

"So where were you hiding?" Rob flung back.

"You growled like an animal," I said.

"I was speaking the bear's language."

Tony glowered at him. "I was on my way back to the bonfire when I heard barking and found Jake in Rob's SUV. Jake pawed the lock button so I was able to open the door. As soon as he was free he bolted in this direction. I've already called Nick. He should be here any minute."

The spray canister dropped from my nerveless fingers. I must have looked as drained as I felt and Tony guided me to a crate to sit down. "You two women should rest a moment. That was a close call."

Shannon hadn't taken her angry eyes off of Rob. "You screamed like an animal."

He waved his hand at her dismissively. "I was trying to distract the bear and save you two nitwits."

I was so tired of the whole evil werewolf thing. Maybe he WAS trying to save us. Nothing made sense and I wanted to be where it was safe. "Shannon, let's go back to the house."

She didn't answer. Her hair was a bright sticky-up nest, her mascara was smudged and she continued to scowl at Rob.

A police siren screeched in the distance. As it grew closer, Rob put his hands over his ears and began to whine like an animal in pain. Soon we could see the flashing red and blue lights through the trees, and when the vehicle pulled up to the edge of the clearing, the siren died, and Nick jumped out. Rob dropped his hands and shook his head, and waited.

"Hi Rob," Nick said and Rob replied confidently. "Constable."

"Is everybody okay?" Nick looked first at Tony, then at Shannon.

"Barely. What took you so long?" Tony said.

Nick pulled a flashlight from his belt and checked the dark parameter of the grove. "Pray the bear is gone. You guys should get out of here."

"It's long gone," Tony said. "Raine's dog chased it away."

"What happened?"

Before anyone else could answer Tony gestured toward Rob. "He saw it all. From the tree. The girls were trapped on the ground. Who knows what could have happened if I hadn't been able to release Jake from Rob's SUV so he could chase it away."

"She had the bear repellant," Rob said. He told Nick what happened, emphasizing that I was the only one with a weapon. Nick glanced at the tree where Rob took refuge. "Don't you know better than to run from a bear? It could have snapped that tree like a twig."

"Well, I, ah.." Rob stuttered, "I expected Raine to use her bear repellant."

Nick allowed his anger to show. "In other words, you thought you were safe in the tree because the bear would go after the girls on the ground, right?"

I enjoyed seeing Rob squirm under the scrutiny of a real alpha guy.

Nick turned to Shannon. "Are you and Raine okay?"

She nodded. "I think so. Adrenalin still on surge."

"Good." Then his manner changed, "I hate to say 'I told you so'...'. But this bonfire idea was more like something Raine would do."

"Hey!" I said.

Shannon straightened and I noted the angry set of her jaw – trauma forgotten. "Are you still mad because I forgot to invite you, officer?"

He stiffened. "Someone could've been badly hurt."

"And how was I to know a bear lurked out here?"

"It was something you should have considered when planning this."

"That's ridiculous," I said. *She should have worried about a werewolf.*

"Come on, Nick. Not the time," Tony said.

"Yeah, Nick," Shannon said, her voice trembling.

We heard something approaching through the trees and then Jake trotted into the clearing. He came straight to me. Of course Tony scratched him like he always did, and even Shannon joined in talking goofy mush. "You saved us you big boy," she said.

Nick's lips formed a slight smile. "Hi, Jake."

Rob cleared his throat. "Actually, he's my dog now. Shannon sold him to me. And you can be sure he will be well rewarded."

Shannon glanced at me. "I'm sorry, Rob. Jake was never my dog to sell." She pulled a wad of cash from her jean pocket. "Here's your money back."

He backed away from her outstretched hand and shook his head. "I want the dog."

Nick took the money from her and held it out to Rob. "I know Jake belongs to Raine. And if he hadn't been trapped in your truck he would have chased the bear away sooner and you wouldn't have had to scrape your arms running up that tree. So why don't you just be a gentleman and forget about it?"

"No. You don't understand. He's may be the last survivor of a rare breed. I want to save his kind by breeding him with my she-wolf. I think I can produce dogs who could help brave men and women such as yourself do their jobs better."

Jake was licking my hand and had not once flicked a glance toward Rob.

"Let's see you get that leash and lead him around," Nick said.

Rob moved fast to grab at the leash, which still dragged from Jake's collar. But Jake managed to dodge him and move out of reach just as he had with the bear. He faced Rob, hackles up, fangs showing.

Rob's lip curled above his canines so fast I wasn't sure what I saw, before his face relaxed into an appeasing smile. "He won't come to me. I haven't started working with him yet."

Nick was expressionless. "Best you go home now. Take the money."

Rob scowled and accepted the cash. "She should be charged with fraud."

"Go home now."

I lifted my chin. "Big Jake would never stay with you anyway. He'd find a way to escape."

Rob put his hands on his hips and gave me a hard stare. His strange yellow eyes still appeared otherworldly. Jake must have sensed it too, because he lunged, teeth snapping inches from the dog trainer's face. For less than a second the air surrounding him rippled as if a warped piece of glass had passed between us, then Rob was standing in a different spot.

I reached for Jake's leash and moved back. Tony's eyes were wide as he met mine. Shannon stepped close to me and clutched my arm. Nick put his hand on his gun. We all sensed something evil.

Rob's eyes dropped to Nick's gun. He said nothing, but simply turned his back and loped out of the clearing. Once the dark had swallowed him up, a long haunting howl broke the silence. Jake threw back his head and answered.

We all exchanged looks of disbelief.

"I think that guy needs a priest," Tony muttered.

No one else said anything about Rob, as if speaking his name would call forth evil. Shannon's face was inscrutable.

"Tony, put out the fire," Nick said at last. "You ladies, in the squad car."

Chapter 32

The doorbell awakened me at 8:30 am.

I threw on my bathrobe and ran fingers through my hair as I made my way to the front door. A balding man in a uniform with a government logo gave me an official smile, and another smile for Jake who sat beside me. After identifying himself as the local Fish and Wildlife Officer, he told me the bear must have returned to the hills. He expressed surprise that it wandered so close to a large gathering of people, but his department was now on alert, should the animal venture back.

"Don't worry, I'm sure he was as afraid of you as you were of him," he declared with too big smile. Then he gestured toward Jake. "Lucky you've got that wolfhound – he'll sense something long before you do. Remember, bears aren't the only dangerous wildlife."

"What else? Wolves, maybe?"

He barked out a jovial laugh. "More like a cougar who's wandered down from the mountains looking for deer, or a coyote after small livestock. Even a doe with a fawn can do a lot of damage with her hooves. But don't concern yourself, we have everything under control."

"Do you worry about domesticated wolves?" I pressed.

"Well, nothing has happened so far, but I guess if a wolf or hybrid got loose, combined with their lack of fear of humans, they might cause trouble. Why? Are you worried about someone?"

He had to know of people like Rob and their pet wolves. Or maybe the government was keeping the lid on sightings of strange beasts to prevent public panic. I realized he was not about to admit to anything so I thanked him for his help and let him leave thinking his department was in control of the situation.

Later, while I munched on toast in the kitchen, Shannon joined me. Jake followed her with a dog-slobbered magazine in his mouth.

"Isn't he cute?" she cooed. "He jumped on the bed and licked my face."

"I think he ruined your magazine," I said.

"You're missing the point. He loves me."

Her favorite baggy pants and "science girl" t-shirt had returned to hide her femininity from the world. But her hair - now a deep auburn, damp and gel-free after her shower – lent her a look of innocence. She went to the fridge and pulled out a big block of cheese, cut off a generous piece, and filled Jake's stuffie. She made him sit while talking in her new annoying baby voice.

I told her what the Wildlife officer said.

"Not new information." She joined me at the island with a cup of coffee.

For several minutes Jake's smacking on his stuffie was the only sound in the kitchen. It started to get on my nerves so I got up to put him outside.

"What are you doing?"

"I thought you didn't like his slurping sounds," I said.

"Leave him alone, he's a hero."

I shrugged. After everything, and the scene last night, I felt rather awkward and wondered which one of us should address the issues between us.

She heaved a sigh of defeat. "I've been a total fool. I don't know if I can get over the humiliation."

I stared at her in surprise.

She looked down.

"Nobody thinks you're a fool. Rob did have a certain magnetism."

"I was the only person who liked him."

"His dog training students worshipped him. Why shouldn't you?"

She didn't respond so I let the silence grow while I wondered if I should bring up the big question on my mind. *Would she have slept with the wolf man?*

"It sure is easy to read your mind."

"Yeah?"

"It gave me some satisfaction to let you think I was going to sleep with him. You were so crazy with that werewolf talk...I admit I tortured you on purpose." She paused. "And I'm really sorry."

I nodded. "I know I sounded crazy. But I was really scared for you."

"I know. And now that I'm back in my right mind, I realize how brave you really were. You even risked your relationship with Tony for me."

"I guess I did," I said. I was beginning to think really highly of myself.

She looked down at her hands, the nails scrubbed clean of the red polish. "Mostly you are so inconsiderate."

Wait. What? "I'm inconsiderate? What about you miss, miss, super bossy brain."

She ignored my outburst. "Rob was so sure of himself; almost invincible. He flattered me with his attention." She paused. "He chose me. Over you. And the more it bugged you, the more I liked him."

"I had no idea you felt competitive toward me," I said.

She got up to make herself some toast. "Let's forget it now."

"Ok. Nick thinks you're pretty."

"You know this based on what evidence?"

"Word on the street. Plus the way he looked at you last night."

She gave a short laugh. "Because I presented my best side."

"He's known you a while. I'm sure he didn't even notice the runny mascara."

"Thanks for the reminder." She thought for a moment. "You know, he's always been conceited, arrogant and...and full of himself. I don't find that attractive."

"Conceited and 'full of himself' mean the same thing," I pointed out.

"Yeah, well, he's REALLY conceited."

We both giggled.

"Anyway, about Rob. Wait here." I ran upstairs for my laptop and returned, plunking it down in front of her.

"What's this?"

"The first day of dog training."

"It doesn't matter now."

"Watch anyway." I clicked on 'play'.

She replayed the video three more times without comment. On the forth run she paused the screen where the shadow became darkest around Rob and Jake jumped into the basin. She stared at it for so long I thought she'd forgotten about me.

"This is probably just a corruption on the file."

I pointed to Jake's image. "He saw something. Dogs see faster motion than we are able to. That's how they communicate with each other without us knowing."

"So?"

"I'm just saying, something surrounds Rob which we can't see but Jake can. And I believe that someday science will be able to measure and acknowledge specters like this."

Her face lit up. "Yes, of course. Ultimately, everything is science. But what about Rob growling in the orchard? And his face changed. You saw it?"

"Everyone did."

"The image on this video must have something to do with it. Did you show this to anyone else?"

"Tony and Aunt Althea."

"And?"

"And she was very shaken. She gave me the pepper spray."

"For Rob?" She gestured to the computer screen, "She thought this would flee from pepper spray?"

"That, and the big book she gave me."

"Poor Rob. He is under the power of something evil. I wish I'd known – it explains everything."

"That's what Tony's aunt said."

"We need to help him."

"She didn't say that! Look, we finally got rid of him. Let's move on. Besides, don't you think he's dangerous?"

"Not if we're careful."

I snorted. "Careful doing what exactly?"

"We have to find someone who has dealt with this sort of thing before." She gestured at the computer screen where she'd frozen the image of Rob and his shadow."

"Argh! This thing is evil. Let's stay away from it."

"What happened to the girl willing to battle a werewolf last night?"

"Her work is done."

"Rob is still in trouble."

"Do you remember the last thing he said to you?"

"He wasn't himself."

I glared at her. "Are you kidding me?"

"He's not a werewolf, Raine. He's a person who needs our help."

Darn. Whenever she got an idea in her head, Shannon could be stubborn. A family trait, I guess. I tilted my head at our dog, chew focused on his toy. "The only protection we have is Jake."

She hopped off her chair to pat Jake on the head. "That's enough because he's my big brave Jakey-Wakey, aren't you sweetie? Yes, you are."

Chapter 33

As we stood in front of the dingy training center door - Shannon, me, and Jake - I had a sense of déjà vu. And not in a good way. I shivered in spite of the heat.

She had assured me that she had no residual feelings for Rob, but simply could not rest knowing an evil entity controlled "the poor guy". "He's a menace to others and to himself," she said and her fervor gave me more insight as to how annoying I must have been. But at least I was happy to let him disappear.

"I still think we should call a priest. Demon stuff is supposed to be their job."

"Quit whining." She pounded on the door and waited for about a minute before she pounded again. She put her ear close to the surface. I watched Jake, knowing his hearing was far superior to ours and his disinterest told me no one was inside. I pointed that out to Shannon and suggested we go home.

She rattled the knob. To our surprise, the door creaked open. "Hello? Rob?" she called.

I stayed behind her. Since she was now on board with the whole evil supernatural creature thing, I let her be the brave one. I would leave it all to her, the oldest and presumably, the smartest.

Jake rushed in and made straight for the basin near the end of the space, remembering the hot dog. We followed, a little more cautiously.

The place appeared to be vacated. The files and papers were gone from the old desk and chairs remained scattered in a loose circle from the last training session - dust thicker than ever. Even the dog odor had faded, overtaken by essence of abandoned building.

"Looks like he's gone," I said.

Shannon strode to the back and pushed the emergency door open to the alley. It was lined with big green bins overflowing with garbage and Jake lost no time lifting his leg on the closest one.

"How's my dog?" The old bottle picker startled us rising up from inside the closest bin, his brown teeth displayed in a wide grin. Jake wagged his tail, then trotted back to me and sat.

"Ah, he wants to stay with you," the man observed. "You must be treating him well."

"Best $30 I ever spent."

"Has he earned his keep?"

Shannon watched him with interest. "He is our guardian angel," she said.

The grin widened. "Ah, the sister who doesn't like dogs. Well, I'm sure happy I'm not feeding the brute." He cackled as he turned back to his dumpster diving.

"Sir," I called, taking a step toward the bin. "Where did you get him? What kind of dog is he?"

"Like your sister said, he's an Angel dog," he said. "Very rare."

"Someone told me he's a Caelum Wolfhound," I persisted.

"He's a mutt little sister. A Muttus Angelus." He snickered at his joke, then sunk into the bin and commenced his rummaging. A pop can came flying out and hit the ground beside his garbage bag.

I hesitated, wanting to know more about my wonderful Jake.

"Never mind Raine, we've got to find Rob."

The 20-minute drive to Rob's home took Shannon less than 10. By the time the car lurched to a stop in front of his property, I swear my finger indentations in the dashboard remained permanent.

A huge padlock secured the gate. Shannon tore down the small piece of cardboard scribbled with the words, 'Keep out. Private

Property' and crumpled it up in frustration. Rob's SUV was not there. Silence in the vicinity of the kennels told us the dogs were gone too.

Instead of staying with us, Jake had galloped over to a large brown dog that lay stretched out on the outside of the chain link fence in the shade of an unkempt azalea bush. I grabbed Shannon's arm and pointed. "That dog is either sick or dead."

Shannon wrinkled her nose. "The poor thing must be sick. I wonder if an epidemic of some dog disease cleared out Rob and his clients?"

"Nothing here seems right." I walked over to it. Jake looked up at me and whined. Flies buzzed around the brown dog's open eyes and its throat was bloody.

I hustled Jake back to the car. I was phoning the SPCA when Nick's police cruiser pulled in behind us. He jumped out and came directly to Shannon's side leaning into the open window so his handsome face was inches from hers.

"What are you ladies doing here?"

We shared a glance. I hoped I didn't appear as guilty as she did.

"You're not selling your dog after all, are you?" he asked.

I assured him that would never happen.

"I'm worried about Rob, actually," Shannon said. "I just wanted to see if he needed help."

Her explanation sounded lame, even to me. Nick regarded her with surprise. "He's a strange one, all right. But what do you think you could do?"

She blushed. "Are you asking as a cop or a friend?"

"Both. I don't want you to get into some kind of trouble and have to call me again."

Shannon smiled sweetly. "What are *you* doing here, Nick? You're not following *us,* are you?"

He returned the smile. "I'm here because I've done some checking into his background and there are some questions..."

I pointed out the dead dog.

He stood up from the window and strode over to it. He gave the poor creature a gentle push with his boot to roll it over. After a moment he came back. "It looks like it was in a dog fight. Maybe a bait dog."

"Is that what you think Rob was into?" I asked, but Shannon shook her head.

"He was all about his business and domesticated wolf breeding program. Dog fighting was the furthest thing from his mind, I'm sure."

We looked at each other and the same thought hit us at the same time. "The wolf killed it," I said.

"Go on home," Nick said. "I'll deal with this." He jogged back to his car.

As we drove away Shannon appeared irritated.

"What?" I said.

"We've known each other since we were kids. Why does he act weird around me?"

"Men, huh?"

"I wonder if Althea is home?"

That was the first idea she'd had that I agreed with. I wanted to clear up a couple of things with Tony's aunt.

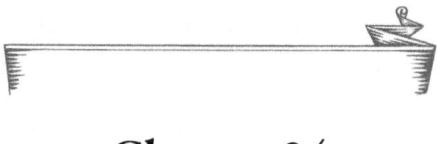

Chapter 34

Shannon parked the car in our driveway, and I ran inside to get *Secrets of the Wolfen* and the Bible to return to her. We went through the orchard, Jake trotting ahead, while I texted Tony. I was happy when he texted back that he was in the veterinarian's clinic with a sheep. We would have Althea all to ourselves perhaps encouraging her to open up more.

We were just about halfway to the house when Jake abruptly stopped, ears pricked, as if he sensed something nearby.

"Jakey-wakey?"

"Is that how I sound?"

She smirked, then grew serious. "Something's weird."

The dog's tail waved slow and high in a dominant position.

"Do you think the bear is back?" I asked.

We both scanned the area. "Walk faster," she said.

Jake stayed right beside us all the way until we reached the fence between the two farms. We heard Sassy barking in the field but Jake did not take off as he normally would.

The late afternoon sun cast shadows everywhere and gave the trees a darkly animated appearance. I hopped over the fence and quickened my step until almost jogging even though I was weighted down by the backpack. Fear adrenalin will do that to a person. Shannon had no trouble keeping up.

We were practically running by the time we arrived at the back gate to the house. Shannon shoved me inside and bolted the lock as soon as Jake was in.

Tony's aunt lounged on a chair under an umbrella by the pool. A silver cross on a long chain rested on her stomach, gleaming against the black of her favorite shirt. Some kind of yellow goop covered her face, with cucumber slices on her eyes and oil shining up her arms and legs. She let us know she was aware of our presence by lifting her hand.

"I don't want to walk home," I said in a low voice and took out my phone to punch in Tony's number. "Nick needs to know the bear may be back."

"That bear wouldn't dare return. We're still spooked from last night and we have to get a hold of ourselves."

The call went to voice mail so I left a message and slid the phone back in my pocket. "Tony can give us a ride home."

We approached Althea while Jake flopped near her under the shade of the umbrella. I took off the backpack and extracted *The Secret Lives of Wolfen* and Bible. "Here are your books," I said. She didn't respond so I placed them on the cement beside her.

"Sit. Food on the table." Her lips barely moved in the center of the mud mask.

Shannon put on a smile. "Nice to meet you. Raine told me you were helpful during this, ah, situation we had."

"The sister," Althea said. "I've been waiting." She did not remove the cucumbers.

We sat and drank, thirsty from the unplanned jog, neither of us sure how to start the conversation.

"What magic is in that facial mask?"

"Old Greek remedy for stress," Althea said, no sign of offense. "Oatmeal and buckwheat honey with lavender oil. Simple and effective."

Bees buzzed close to her edible face while I considered asking her what was causing her stress. One of them landed on her nose. She let out a squawk and sat up faster than I could have predicted an old lady to move, swiping at the bee. The cucumbers plopped onto the cement while she jumped around the lounge chair and flailed her hands at an invisible swarm. Jake leaped up out of the way and moved a few feet away onto the grass. She didn't sit down again for several seconds.

"Those stupid bees," she muttered. "I told them yesterday to go."

I handed her a cloth from the table. "They're are attracted to the honey and lavender."

She snatched it from me. "I know this."

Nobody spoke as she wiped the goop off her face. I noticed the tall pink hollyhocks she had placed in column vases on either side of the back door. She seemed to appreciate the aesthetic value of flowers as much as their so-called wolf repellant properties. I remembered the same flowers somewhere else - up around the picker's cabin and was about to tell her about them when something else came to mind.

That day I met her on the way to the Callas farm, a few hollyhocks were mixed in with her cuttings of foxglove and lupine. She must have been coming from the cabin.

I gasped. "You took the lamb."

She stiffened.

"Raine, don't be silly," Shannon said. "Why would she steal her own nephew's lamb?

"I don't know. Why would you, Althea?"

She said nothing, not even any outrage at the accusation. I remembered the conversation I had with Rob after the bear attack.

"Rob didn't know anything about that fur talisman buried in the ground either. That's because you put it there."

She avoided my eyes, her body stiff with guilt. "I had my reasons."

"Were you working up more spells?"

"Something like that."

Shannon leaned toward her, a hard look in her eyes. "Please stop playing my sister and tell her what's going on. She's been so worried. You owe her an explanation."

Althea sighed. "I heard the howling. If I merely told you I sensed evil, you children would have laughed it off. I did those other things to get your attention." She folded her arms with resolve. "You needed to take the threat seriously. The curse, the evil is real."

"Tony was completely stressed about his flock," I said.

"Are you listening? The threat is not gone."

"By 'threat' do you mean werewolf?" Shannon said.

"Wolfen. The thing behind the man."

"If the evil is still around, what are we supposed to do?" I asked.

She turned away. Defeated, like she didn't know. When she observed my disappointment, she hoisted herself up and snatched *The Secret Lives of Real Werewolves* from beside her chair. "You read this?"

I nodded.

"You know as much as I do. Don't go anywhere without your dog. And ask Nick for help. I'll do what I can from here." She nodded toward the Bible. "You may still need that," and left it by her chair. She walked back into the house slightly hunched over, hugging the book to her chest.

"Is she trying to scare us again?" I said. "Why ask Nick for help?"

Shannon thought for a moment. "Because he has a gun."

After a few minutes we heard Tony's truck. He entered the back yard without surprise at our presence, Sassy at his side, and stopped to pat Jake. He slid into a chair beside me and the dogs flopped in the shade by the table.

I told Tony about Althea's role in the strange events of the past few days. He did not react as outraged as I thought he would. "Considering how eccentric she is, I should have suspected her."

"She wasn't entirely wrong about Rob, though."

"Nick is pretty sure he already left town."

"He needs help." Shannon sighed, drawing a grimace of impatience from Tony.

"I guess that's one way of looking at it."

The sun was low in the sky – supper time - so Tony ordered pizza delivery and by the time it arrived daylight had faded into dusk. Nick showed up right behind the pizza dressed in long shorts and t-shirt, having finished his shift for the day. As soon as I saw him I asked about the dead dog.

"The SPCA removed it and is investigating. It didn't have any tags or microchip so it must have been a stray. Maybe Rob did let his wolf at it. So your friend..." he looked at Shannon. "is wanted for questioning. It seems he's missing."

"As much as I don't like Rob, I can't think why he would allow a dog to be killed," I said. I wondered if Jake had come close. Sensing my thoughts, Tony reached from my hand and squeezed it reassuringly and I squeezed back.

Nick shrugged. "Maybe he didn't but he could know something or have seen someone. So why would he leave so suddenly if he had nothing to hide?"

"A coincidence," Shannon said.

He pulled a chair up next to her. "You don't still have feelings for him, do you?"

She lifted her chin. "My feelings for him were superficial."

He straightened and reached for the last slice of pizza. "Maybe I should thank you two. If Shannon hadn't been involved with him, I would never have investigated his background. Turns out, he used to live in Toronto and his real name is Roger Colby. He's a person of interest in a number of dog mutilations between Toronto and Mississauga."

"The Rob I know admired dogs. He wanted Jake for breeding purposes," Shannon said. "How do you know this Roger Colby is Rob?"

"A pretty accurate investigative trail," he replied. "I'm sure he's long gone but I'm going to keep checking to see if a weird dog trainer shows up anywhere else."

Shannon didn't want to believe the worst of Rob yet. "Poor Rob. His dreams are ruined if he's got law enforcement already sure he's a criminal."

"You do still care about him," Nick said.

"As a human being!"

She stood up, her cheeks flushed. "Come on Raine, I'm ready to leave."

I grabbed the backpack and then put the Bible in it, I didn't really know why.

"Maybe Tony could give us a ride?" I suggested, although judging by Shannon's stormy expression, not likely.

"Don't be such a baby. It's a 10-minute walk and we've got Jake if you're scared."

"I don't mind," Tony said.

Nick stood up jingling the keys to his car. "I'll take you."

"Raine can go with you if she wants." She stalked toward the gate and Jake followed her, but his tail was down and he didn't look happy. I realized two things: One, he wanted to protect her; and two, he sensed something out there that she needed protection from. Not comforting.

"I'll go with you," Tony said to me.

"Thanks, but I don't want you to walk back alone," I said.

"I can stay over night," he said with a hopeful smile.

Nick chuckled. "I can drive you ladies. Simple."

"We have been walking back and forth through that orchard for years," Shannon said. "Let's go."

Nick sat down again, exasperated. "Bullheadedness doesn't become you, Shannon. The only reason I'm letting you go is because I know the bear is back in the hills – Fish and Wildlife tracked it. And you've got Jake."

That earned him another chilly look.

Tony took two minutes to retrieve a lantern from the house and when he returned Shannon was holding the gate open. "Jake protected us once, he can do it again."

Chapter 35

A bright moon lit the clear sky, just like the night before, and I was filled with an unexplainable sense of dread. All four of us hurried across the Callus's property and over the fence into our orchard with the same sense of urgency, Jake leading the way, head up and tail down. Tony's lantern illuminated too narrow a path. Anything could be lurking in the shadows only feet away.

No one spoke until finally the porch light on our house came into view, twinkling through the branches of the trees, and I breathed a sigh of relief.

"Faster," Shannon ordered, her voice carrying in the quiet of the evening.

We were already moving as fast as possible without wearing ourselves out before we reached safety and I told her so. At that point the fear on her face reminded me again of the dream I'd had the night Rob cased our orchard with his wolf. The scent of grass and the gloom that engulfed me were exactly the same.

I pulled my hair hoping this was another nightmare but I did not wake up in bed.

She glanced over her shoulder. "I swear those shadows are alive."

"It's the way the lantern is moving," Tony said.

I caught the shifting shapes as well. "Everything is the same as a nightmare I had the other night when Rob's wolf was howling. Except you weren't in it, Tony. I hope that's a good sign."

"We're almost there and no bloodthirsty creatures yet."

A faint howl from the other side of the hill disturbed the peace. Shannon jumped and grabbed my hand. Jake tensed, his tail high.

"Now will you walk faster?" she hissed.

We had advanced a few feet when an otherworldly wailing started up not far away. At first hollow and quiet, the sound gained momentum in a clamor of keening, moaning and crying, only one voice but just as chilling as the many voices in the dream.

Jake responded with a challenging howl.

"Run!" Tony shouted.

We ran, Tony pulling me by the hand and Shannon a few steps ahead. We hadn't gone but a couple of yards before the light from the lantern reflected two unnatural glowing yellow eyes inside the dark outline of a huge four-legged creature. We stopped short. A deep growl arose from Jake's chest.

"Jake," I said, my teeth chattering.

The beast began to circle us, a quiet hair raising sound emanating from within it.

Shannon drew a quick breath. "Rob's wolf."

The beast uttered a soft groan and then, terrifyingly, stood up on two legs. The eerie eyes bobbed with the great head as it lurched toward us.

I rasped, "Run, run, run." But my limbs would not move like in the dream.

Jake sprung at the beast, and it went down on all fours snarling with rage. Tony swung the lantern and managed to glance off its flank, drawing a snarl even as it remained focused on Jake.

The beast was as tall as Jake but heavier muscled and fast – supernaturally fast like Rob. My fear for Jake overtook my concern for personal safety and I rushed forward, blindly flailing the heavy backpack. I managed a glancing blow on the wolf's back and Tony struck with the lantern on its head as it lunged at Jake. Jake yelped but scampered away, trying to draw it away from us.

"He's going to kill my dog." With tears flowing I clenched my jaw and swung the backpack again, striking the beast on the nose. It howled in pain and then turned and fastened its malevolent yellow eyes on mine. As the blood pounded in my head, the sound of the beast's own panting surrounded me, hot and terrifying.

It knocked me to the ground and the air left my lungs. With one paw on my chest it held me down and it's great teeth gleamed above my head, hell rolling up from its chest as it lowered its gaping jaws and saliva dripped onto my face. I couldn't cry or call out, I couldn't breath. I heard both Shannon and Tony screaming.

At that moment a thunderous growl rolled over us like a tsunami of sound waves. It sounded like it came from the sky. Then Jake lunged at the wolf and grabbed onto its throat. The beast roared and began thrashing its head to shake him off but Jake's jaws seemed locked in a vise-like grip. The two began to move together in a circle, Jake hanging on, even though the size and strength of the wolf seemed certain to win this fight.

As they tumbled together, the carnage was almost impossible to follow in the gloom yet we could see, caught in the light of the lantern, the glistening of blood on the ground.

I was close enough to inhale the awful smell of animal musk and the rotten egg odor of sulfur rolled together into one overpowering stench. I gulped in some air and Tony and Shannon helped me to my feet, pulling me away from the battle.

"Come on, let's go!" Tony yelled.

"We must go," Shannon cried and tried to pull me away, but I couldn't go.

"I can't leave Jake to die," I said and shook her off.

"He'll be okay. He's got the wolf by the throat," Shannon said, her voice raised against the hideous din of snarling. Overwhelmed with despair, I could only hope she was right.

Tony raised the lantern in hopes of landing another blow on the wolf but the two animals were moving too fast. The artificial light cast his pale face in an eerie glow.

Once the wolf was able to shake the dog loose, in a nanosecond it was on top, one of its great paws pinning Jake's head.

I don't know what sounded first, my horrified scream or the boom of a gun, but in the next moment there was an inhuman cry of pain. As he wailed, the wolf's eyes looked right into mine, then he turned and fled, one of his back legs dangling. Another crack of the gun followed him. We couldn't tell if it hit its mark but the wailing and crying continued for a long time before fading into the black distance.

I turned just as Nick stepped up behind Tony, his rifle raised toward the dark. "Is everyone okay?" he asked as he slowly lowered it.

Shannon held my hand. "Raine?"

I pulled from her grasp and ran to Jake who watched the dark as if he could see. "Jakey!" Tony brought the lantern up over the dog so I could examine him. Blood spatters covered his fur but as I ran my hand over his sides and legs, I could not find any wounds. He wagged his tail and licked my hand.

"I think we're okay," Tony said.

"Good," Nick said crisply. "Let's get up to the house."

He cradled the rifle, ready to be aimed. He made us walk in single file with Tony and Jake in front, and Nick guarding the rear. None of us spoke until we got into the house. We all flopped down in the kitchen, everyone looking as exhausted as I felt.

"This is one time I'm glad you followed us," Shannon said to Nick. "You saved us. And Jake."

"It was Althea's idea. She insisted that I follow you. When I hesitated she yelled at me. I wasn't going to argue." He nodded at Jake who was lying on the floor at my feet, his fur matted and full of dirt and grass. "That is quite the dog. I hate to think about what would have happened had he not been with you."

Tony looked at me. "Me too."

"There are no words," Shannon agreed and as if he knew they were talking about him, Jake's tail thumped on the floor.

"What are you going to do now?" I asked.

"A wolf in an agricultural area is a matter for Fish and Wildlife to deal with," Nick said. "I will contact them."

"So that's it, then?" I said. "Shouldn't the residents around here be alerted that there could be a...dangerous wolf in the area?"

Nick looked uncomfortable and did not answer right away, drawing a frown from Shannon. "Well, Nick? You had to fire your gun. The animal, whatever it is, is dangerous."

"Yes, yes. I'm sure notices will be sent out to the surrounding farmers. But you guys don't have to worry about it tonight."

Tony stood up. "I agree with Nick. You need to get some rest, Raine. You look all in. Nick and I will be going."

"No, no. You can't walk back tonight. It's too dangerous," I said.

Nick glanced at Shannon and a small smile played on his lips. "I agree. Tonight we're staying here. Best for everyone."

Tony perked up. "Good idea."

I admit, I liked the thought of Tony sleeping in my house all night, even though a whole level would separate us. I didn't think we were in danger in the house with Jake on guard, but I was not about to send the two men back outside tonight.

Shannon was uncomfortable but she couldn't send them out either. "There's a spare bed and pull-out sofa that's quite comfortable downstairs."

I dragged myself out of the chair and went to get some blankets. When I handed them over to Tony. He was tired too and could only offer half a smile. But I was so glad he was there that I kissed him quick on the lips.

"Save that for tomorrow," he murmured. I felt the thrill of promise re-engergize me and ran back upstairs.

The next morning I awakened to the smell of coffee and a bright sun ripening the apples in the orchard. I had slept soundly, rather miraculously, considering the trauma and adrenaline working overtime the night before. I should have been more traumatized by the danger and violence we had encountered but I wasn't. I knew I wasn't in shock either. The one reason I was okay, both physically and mentally – Jake. My Muttus Angelus.

A quiet tap on the door completely cleared my head as Shannon stepped in, deep concern on her face. "Are you okay? Really?"

"Yes."

"I mean, there was a giant wolf on top of you..."

"We were all traumatized," I said. "But now we're all okay and I'm pretty sure Rob is gone and we're safe with Jake."

"And Nick," she said.

"Okay. You'd better thank him a lot and be nice to him from now on," I said.

"Yes."

"Why have you always been so grumpy to him, anyway?" I asked.

She shrugged. "He's always been so full of himself."

"He wants to impress you."

She looked surprised. "Do you think so?"

"Look, Shannon. While you've been studying science, I've been studying biology."

She laughed and threw a pillow at me. "Get dressed."

Knowing Tony and I would be having breakfast together added some cheer to the morning. After a quick shower I put on my prettiest blouse with pink shorts and went downstairs.

Everyone else was already up. A big plate of scrambled eggs – Tony's contribution – sat in the center of the island beside an also big plate of bacon. When Tony spied me he gestured to a place setting at the kitchen island.

"Hurry up, Sleeping Beauty, or Nick will eat yours too."

I took a seat as he slid eggs onto my plate. "When you guys walk back I'm coming too," I said. "I want to see the area where it attacked us."

"Me too," Shannon said.

Nick shook his head. "It might come back."

"No it won't," I said, "Not in the daytime and probably not ever again."

"How do you know?" Shannon said.

Quietly Tony said. "We'll ask Aunt Althea."

NICK BROUGHT HIS RIFLE and the four of us plus dog ventured out to examine the battle area. It was easy to find – the disturbance in dirt and grass, fur clumps, and huge paw prints, plus a blood trail leading off through the orchard heading north toward the hills was hard to miss. Our own intermingling footprints and tracks and those of Jake's were visible and the backpack lay where I'd dropped it. I hoisted it onto my shoulders, feeling the solidity of the book inside.

"Be careful," Nick warned. "Fish and Wildlife is going to be here soon so don't disturb anything."

He watched Jake who was sniffing around the area, no sign of tension.

"If there was anything around here right now Jake would not be so relaxed," Tony said.

"If that wolf is still loose Rob is looking for him." Shannon said. "That animal was very important to him."

There wasn't much else to say and only one noisy magpie and the whirring of a few grasshoppers filled the silence.

"Hey, look who's here," Tony said. His aunt approached from the hill with a basket of freshly picked hollyhocks.

"Hey, did anyone let her know?" Shannon asked, looking at the guys. Nick nodded. "I called her after you went to bed."

When she reached us she studied the area as if she could see something we couldn't.

"What did you see last night?" she asked.

"A big black wolf," I said. "It attacked us like it was...personal."

She patted Jake. "It was."

"Why?" Shannon said.

She shrugged and kept stroking Jake. "Your angel is powerful. I wasn't really sure about your dog until last night. The wolfen had to get rid of the dog because he guarded you and your sister."

"Are you saying the werewolf was after Shannon after all?" I asked.

"Both of you."

"Why did the, er, wolfen want us?" Shannon asked.

Althea seemed embarrassed. "What? You think I am God that I know everything? Nobody knows why maidens have been disappearing for centuries."

That stopped conversation for a few beats. I knew Shannon and Tony were no longer skeptics regarding werewolves. How could they be?

"Do you think Rob is a werewolf?" Shannon asked her.

"If he's smart, Rob is far away by now," Nick muttered. "I'm going to be tracing him."

"Don't go looking for him," Althea warned. She turned back toward the Callas' property. Tony called her to wait, but she waved without turning.

He sighed and took my hand. "Let's do something normal today like the lake. And not analyze werewolves and angels for a while."

"I'm up for that."

He bent toward me and I moved closer, my heart racing, as we leaned in for our first kiss.

Nick clapped his brother on the back, interrupting us. "Great idea! I've got the day off – I know this little hidden cove where we can have some privacy."

I glanced Shannon's way. She watched Nick, her expression unreadable.

As we walked home behind them Tony spoke low so that only I could hear. "Is there something going on between those two?"

I gave him a pained look. "I am so finished speculating on Shannon's love life."

She did seem to be walking closer to Nick with her head tilted ever so slightly toward him. I couldn't hear what he was saying. He spoke low, for her ears only.

Tony tightened his hold on my hand and did that light brushing thing with his thumb. How could such a simple touch send such a thrill all the way to the core of my being?

Jake, who had been following quietly behind Tony and me, whined. I turned around. He had stopped and was looking as if he was trying to tell me something. Then he turned and stared off into the orchard, ears forward.

"What's wrong, Jakey-Wakey?"

Shannon and Nick kept walking oblivious to anything beyond their new awareness of each other.

I scanned the orchard, alert for lurking creatures. The thick fruit-laden trees were awash in the midday sun and innocent of menace.

Following Jake's line of vision Tony pointed through the trees. "I think someone is there."

Then I saw a figure emerge from behind a pile of crates and make his way toward us. Jake gave a single bark, his tail wagging. The old man waved.

"Who is that?" Tony said.

Jake looked from me to the old man and whined again. A lump formed in my throat. "Jake's true partner," I said.

When he reached us he smiled and this time he was not really old or dirty. His eyes looked into mine. "You ladies are okay now?" he said. It wasn't really a question.

Jake licked my hand. A tear rolled down my cheek.

"How...?" Tony stared at me.

"Goodbye, Jake," I whispered.

I swear the dog wanted to say something and maybe if we waited long enough, he would have. But the old man spoke instead, "Come on, old friend." He turned and started walking away. Jake licked my hand one more time before following.

"Hey!" Tony said. "He's taking your dog."

"Jake is my friend and angel, but he was never my dog," I said. As we watched, the two made their way back toward the pile of crates and behind it. Then we couldn't see them anymore.

Tony gently wiped the tear from my cheek. "I'm sorry for everything...for giving you such a hard time," he said.

I wrapped my arms around him and pressed my face to his chest. "I want you to kiss me," I said to the chest.

"What?"

I pulled away and looked into his kind wonderful eyes. "I want you to kiss me."

He did not smile. Instead, he cupped his hands around my face and kissed me. I moved into him and kissed him back. We stood there together for a long time.

Epilogue

"**Y**our nephew shot the werewolf and survived?" Cricket said, admiration shining in her eyes. "Magnificent! Aunt, your 7th Sense is back, and it protected him."

She patted Althea's trembling hands, folded in her lap. The old lady sat in a great armchair surrounded by her three fussing friends in her tiny apartment above the *Friendly Potions Shop*. The pungent odour of fresh pine permeated the tidy and prettily furnished sitting room, caught in the warmth of the sunlight from the big front window. The traffic and street sounds below seemed distant, as if in another world.

Althea frowned, recalling the whole event. "I worry about Nick."

Cricket exchanged a look with her sisters. "I flew down a couple of times to make sure you were okay. Nick is very strong. Maybe he inherited..."

"Don't." Althea warned. "My whole family thinks I'm crazy now."

"They always thought you were crazy, dear," Marian said, earning a frown from Cricket.

"Did you bring back any fruit?" Georgine asked, and when no one answered, she went into the kitchen to look.

Althea sighed and she rested her head in her hand. "My 7th Sense is almost gone. I can't do anything right. I couldn't banish the wolfen spirit. I was even attacked by bees."

Cricket's brow furrowed in puzzlement. "You put out the wolf's fur and the lamb to confuse the beast, correct?"

"Yes."

"The wolfen couldn't harm the girls because of your spells. He couldn't kill the dog. They worked, Aunt."

"Don't be foolish," Althea snapped. "He couldn't kill the dog because of the dog. And something else."

"What?" Marian asked.

"I don't know. Yet."

Georgine hopped back into the room with a bowl of cherries. "I liked the 'bear repellent' you prepared for the wolfen. Nice touch."

But Althea only frowned. "The girl never used it. I don't even know if it would have worked."

"That always happens," Marian said, sympathetically.

"The point is, you did what you could," Cricket said. "Everything worked out, and at least you helped."

Georgine stopped smacking on a cherry and held up a hand, her eyes unnaturally large and fixed on something only she could see. The others watched her with alarm.

Agitated, she waved a cherry by its stem until it flew off and hit the window.

"Althea is right. There is something else."

Don't miss out!

Visit the website below and you can sign up to receive emails whenever Jayna James publishes a new book. There's no charge and no obligation.

https://books2read.com/r/B-A-SQIZ-XFJLC

BOOKS 2 READ

Connecting independent readers to independent writers.

About the Author

Jayna James lives in Southern Alberta with her husband and a tiny dog.